PRAMA

Also by **JAMIE PONTI**

Animal Attraction

PRAMA

JAMIE PONTI

Simon Pulse
New York London Toronto Sydney

SIMON PULSE
An imprint of Simon & Schuster
Children's Publishing Division
1230 Avenue of the Americas, New York, NY 10020
Copyright © 2008 by James Ponti
All rights reserved, including the right of reproduction
in whole or in part in any form.
SIMON PULSE and colophon are registered trademarks
of Simon & Schuster, Inc.
Designed by Mike Rosamilia
The text of this book was set in Adobe Garamond.
Manufactured in the United States of America
First Simon Pulse edition February 2008
10 9 8 7 6 5 4 3 2 1
Library of Congress Control Number 2007937612
ISBN-13: 978-1-4169-6100-0
ISBN-10: 1-4169-6100-3

For Grayson

ACKNOWLEDGMENTS

Although this is a work of fiction, there are some very real people who helped make it happen. I have endless gratitude for the Prama Queens of Simon Pulse—Jennifer Klonsky and Bethany Buck. I had the great pleasure of learning the latest in prom etiquette from the best and the brightest of Winter Park High School. The lovely Heather Croteau was always eager to read and offer suggestions. And my family put up with late hours and grumpy moods well above and beyond the normal call of duty. Most of all, I would like to thank Denise, who not only is a great editor, but is also the coolest person I know.

Molly Jeanine Walker
Girl's Soccer 10, 11; Honor Society 11, 12;
Student Council 11; French Club 11;
Yearbook 11, 12; Prom Committee, chair 12
"If we cannot find a road to success, we
will build one."

Allison Marie Pirlo
Girl's Soccer 10, 11, 12; Band 10, 11, 12;
Prom Committee 12
"Toto, I've got a feeling we're not in
Kansas anymore."

Rachel Leigh Buchanan—"Most Original"
Newspaper Staff 10, 11, editor 12;
Girl's State 11; Band 10, 11, 12;
Homecoming Court 12; Honor Society 11, 12
"So we beat on, boats against the current,
borne back ceaselessly into the past."

Victoria Marie Sligh—"Most Popular"
Cheerleading, 10, 11, captain 12; Senior Class
President 12; Homecoming Court 11, queen 12;
Honor Society 11, 12; Beta Club 10, 11, 12
"Second place is the first loser."

Jenna Marie Copeland—"Most Fashionable"
Cheerleading 11, 12; Senior Class Vice
President 12; Homecoming Court 12;
Honor Society 11, 12; Beta Club 10, 11, 12
"Fashion comes and goes; style is forever."

Karolina Olsen—"Most Beautiful"
Student Government 12; Homecoming Court 12;
Chess Club 12; Interact 12; International Club 12
*"Man märker andras fel och
glömmer sina egna."*

Matthew James Hall—"Most Athletic"
Football 10, 11, captain 12; Basketball
10, 11, captain 12; Baseball 10, 11,
captain 12; Fellowship of Christian
Athletes 10, 11, 12; Homecoming Court 12
"I never meant 2 cause U any sorrow . . .
I never meant 2 cause U any pain . . ."

Benjamin Bauer (West High School)
Swimming 12; School News Reporter 12
"You can't always get what you want, but
if you try sometimes, well you just might
find, you get what you need."

Peter Thomas McLaurin
Yearbook 12; Interact 11, 12
"I am McLovin'."

Charles "Chas" Montgomery—"Most Studious"
Chess Club 9, 10, 11, vice president 12;
National Honor Society 10, 11, 12;
Gamers Club 11, 12; Science Fair 11, 12
"I can calculate the motions of heavenly
bodies, but not the madness of people."

Warren Clyde Sadler
Band 10, 11, 12
"Are we having fun yet?"

John Cameron Warfield
Yearbook 12; Beta Club 11, 12
"For those about to rock, we salute you!"

pra·ma // [**prah**-*muh*, **pram**-*uh*] *noun*

1. prom drama

2. a situation or series of events related to one's prom and marked by emotional outbursts, paranoid overreactions, and feelings of tremendous insecurity

Usage: *When Jessica learned the dress wasn't available with an empire waist, she sobbed uncontrollably, displaying classic symptoms of prama.*

chapter ONE

Whenever an adult asked her what she wanted to be, Molly Walker always answered "forensic pathologist." This was a total lie—she got ill at the thought of dissecting a frog, much less a person. But it sounded cool and usually made them stop asking annoying questions.

Molly's actual interest in forensic pathology was limited to her obsessive devotion to crime-scene television shows. Each one started with some gorgeous hooker or hot millionaire lying facedown in an expensive bathroom. The thing she loved about the shows was that the bodies were always being examined by a brainy member of the coroner's staff who both the hooker and millionaire would have totally ignored if they had all gone to the same school. In these shows, good things happened to smart people and bad things happened to beautiful people.

In other words, it was the exact opposite of high school.

Molly also loved the women on these shows. They were smart and sexy and didn't take shit from anybody. In her heart of hearts, she wished she could radiate the same kind of cool-girl persona.

Just the thought of it made her laugh.

She was wrapping up a week that was anything but cool. It started with her boyfriend dumping her, continued with her bombing major tests in both English and trig, and was culminating in a freak heat wave that made it so humid she could literally feel her hair curling as she waited for a traffic light to change. (Typically, curly hair wasn't on the same level as heartbreak and bad grades, but since it was prom day, her hair had heightened importance.)

The heat wave had arrived just in time to ruin her prom picture. Now, in some dusty frame on a shelf in the den, she'd have frizzy unkempt hair for the rest of eternity. (If only she wore her old retainer and cat's-eye glasses, she could have completed the ensemble.)

She checked the rearview mirror and gasped at the tangled mess on top of her head. It was worse than she thought. It didn't help that the car's air conditioner was broken. Riding around town with the windows down only made it worse.

The long-dead air conditioner was just one of many things wrong with Molly's car, an ancient Volvo now on its third generation in the Walker family. It had been neon blue when her grandmother first picked it out at the dealership. Now, nineteen years later, it was the color of an old pair of jeans. Except for the passenger-side door, which was the color of a brand-new pumpkin. (Orange was the only color available at the junkyard after a particularly poor attempt at parallel parking.)

The floorboard was held together with duct tape and had a hole in it the size of a quarter. This meant Molly's left shoe got wet whenever it rained. She had no delusions about its life expectancy. As a rule, she never put in more than six dollars of gas at any one time because she didn't want to waste a full tank when it took its inevitable trip to the Volvo graveyard.

Despite all of this—or perhaps because of it—Molly *loved* the car. Every great memory she had of high school was somehow connected to it. It had carried her and her friends to countless football games, provided privacy for endless talks, and was the scene of more than a few romantic highlights.

The car was such an essential part of Molly's life that even the most junior forensic tech on one of her shows could create a complete profile of her just by looking at clues from the vehicle.

The trunk housed her collected letters—in it you could find crumpled up homework, term papers, and even some random love notes dating back to sophomore year. They painted a picture of a girl who made good if not stellar grades and who could pen a righteous love letter, but not always muster up the courage to send it.

The glove compartment was filled with mix CDs she'd made during various stages of her musical maturation. They showed an evolution that went from rock to reggae to country to emo and back to rock again.

The trickiest clue to decipher was the gooey residue on the rear window. It marked where there once had been a Princeton University sticker. (Molly ripped it off moments after getting the rejection letter in the mail.)

She hoped the car would make it all the way to graduation, and not just for sentimental reasons. She hated the idea of bumming rides to all those end-of-the-year parties and events. Now, though, she thought she'd be lucky if it lasted through the night.

As it rattled down the street, an altogether new and mysterious noise started coming from the engine. It was a grinding noise. Molly didn't know much about cars, but she assumed grinding noises were bad.

At best, the car needed another trip to the mechanic, which she couldn't afford. At worst, it was time to put it out of its misery. Either way, it demanded instant attention. *Instant attention*, however, was something she just couldn't manage. Not today. She had way too many things to worry about. So, she did the only sensible thing she could think of. She reached over to the radio and turned up the volume until the music drowned out the grinding. Maybe, she reasoned, if she didn't hear it, it would just go away.

That's the kind of day she was having.

It wasn't even ten and she was already on her fifth Red Bull. This broke the record she set the day she retook the SAT. Unfortunately, it hadn't helped much then and didn't seem to be helping now.

Amazingly, the car made it all the way to the American Legion hall without breaking down. She pulled into the parking lot and brought it to a loud and merciful stop. Before getting out, she closed her eyes and took a long, deep breath. If caffeine and sugar weren't going to work, maybe meditation would do the trick.

She was able to meditate for all of three and a half seconds before the peace and quiet were interrupted.

"Nice hair," the voice came from beside her. "I think a blue jay is building a nest in back."

Molly smiled and opened her eyes to see her best friend, Allison, standing by the car. "Thanks," Molly replied. "Anything I can do to help the environment."

Molly got out of the car and the two of them headed for the door.

"How many is that?" Allison asked, pointing at the silver-and-blue can in Molly's hand.

"Two," Molly answered.

Allison just gave her a look.

"Okay, five," Molly admitted.

Allison took a deep breath. "This should be fun."

This was the final meeting of the prom committee. The first had taken place during the second week of school. That's when Molly had been elected prom committee chair.

She won in a landslide. Mostly because no one else wanted it. She couldn't have cared less. It was a job she was born to do. Her motivation was simple. She wanted to make sure her prom didn't suck. She'd gone as a junior and found it beyond lame. She was going to make sure that her class went out strong.

Molly had tackled the job with great enthusiasm. She'd orchestrated six fund-raisers, oversaw bimonthly theme meetings, and auditioned dozens of bands and deejays without so much as once losing her sense of humor or sanity. But now, with the end in sight, she felt that grip loosening.

Like her car, she wasn't quite sure she could make it.

The first cracks had appeared the night before when she got bitchy at the end of a grueling nine-hour decorate-a-thon. There was simply too much to do and too few people to do it.

That hadn't always been the case. At one time, the prom committee had enough people to polish off a dozen pizzas after a meeting. But, like most high school groups, the membership plummeted after the yearbook picture was taken and really thinned out once the hard work kicked in.

There was also what Allison dubbed "the Battle of Moulin Rouge."

It happened during a meeting in which a girl with a total Nicole Kidman fixation demanded that "Moulin Rouge" be selected as the prom theme. The idea started to build some support until it was squashed by a group of boys who refused to be a part of anything (as they put it) "so freaking lame."

To make matters worse, they wanted the theme to be "It's Vegas, Baby!" (It didn't help that the boy leading the Vegas group had once dated and dumped the Nicole wannabe.)

The argument that followed was very loud and extremely petty. It had plenty of yelling and crying and even some minor head trauma when she pelted him with a hardback copy of *The Grapes of Wrath*.

"It's amazing he lived," Allison said later when she checked the back of the book and discovered it was 1,067 pages long.

When the dust settled and the final vote was cast, neither "Moulin Rouge" nor "It's Vegas, Baby!" was selected. The surprise winner was "Hollywood Dreams," which caused both of the other groups to storm out and quit.

Now the committee was down to eight diehards, all of them girls and three named Michelle. Each one was as bleary-eyed and caffeine-addled as Molly.

The purpose of the meeting was simple. Molly needed to take one final walk-through of the hall to make sure that everything was officially *prom ready*. She had a clipboard with a checklist, and once she gave the committee the word, they could finally stop planning the big night and start enjoying it.

Despite being overworked, the group had done an amazing job transforming the building into a Hollywood dreamland.

This had been no easy task. After all, drab olive walls were fine for the clogging festival, but prom was prom. These memories were supposed to last a lifetime.

Along one wall, they'd built a replica of the Hollywood sign that looked just like the real thing. (Actually, the father of one of the Michelles built it, but it had taken all of them to assemble it and put it up.) Another wall was covered with classic movie posters like *Casablanca* and *Gone with the Wind*. The floor had stars just like the ones on the Walk of Fame—except rather than celebrities' names, these had the names of their classmates.

Molly walked around with her clipboard and checklist while the other girls sprawled out on the red carpet that was for the grand entry. It wasn't really supposed to be a meeting, just a quick formality. But the girls started to get nervous when they saw that Molly was taking notes. When she finally stopped, she came back over to them.

Even Allison wasn't quite sure what was going on in Molly's head. "So?" she asked. "What do you think?"

"I think it's amazing," Molly answered.

The girls heaved a collective sigh of relief.

"Amazing, that I didn't realize this earlier," she continued. "The Hollywood sign is all wrong. I can say it because it was my idea, but it's way too cheesy."

One of the Michelles started to twitch, but this didn't slow Molly one bit. She wasn't so much talking to them as she was having a conversation with herself.

"And these stars," she said, pointing at the floor. "I think we need to get a ruler and check the alignment. They just seem . . . wrong."

Allison didn't like where this was headed. She had a quick flashback to the Battle of Moulin Rouge. Only this time her best friend was leading the suicide mission.

Molly kept rolling. "Now, about the balloon drop, I've been doing some new calculations, and considering the square footage of the dance floor and the number of balloons, we are way too—"

She never got to finish her algebraic equation. Allison just grabbed her and dragged her straight to the bathroom. When they got inside, Allison locked the door behind them and turned on all of the faucets so that no one could listen in.

"I wasn't ready for the bathrooms," Molly said, not missing a beat. "But since we're here, I think we could spruce this up a bit too."

"Do you hear what you're saying?" Allison asked. She waved her hand in front of Molly's face, trying to break her out of her trance.

Molly stalled for a second and went to take another hit of Red Bull. Allison snapped the can out of her hand and poured it down the drain.

"Look at yourself," Allison demanded.

Molly looked in the mirror for a moment and gasped, "Oh my God!"

"Exactly," Allison replied, thinking she'd gotten through.

"My hair is getting worse!"

"Can I get a little focus?" Allison shot back. "You are freaking out."

"I am doing no such thing," Molly said defensively. "This is our prom. It needs to be right. I have spent months planning this thing, and it's going to be perfect."

"Listen Molls," Allison said. "I love you to death. You know that. And that's why I can tell you that you are full-on geekin' at the worst possible time. These girls have slaved for you and it's over. There is no such thing as perfect."

"I just had a couple of small—"

"Done!" Allison said emphatically.

Molly took another look in the mirror and sighed. "You're right," she said with a nod.

"Of course I'm right," Allison said with a wry smile. "I'm always right."

Molly gave her a skeptical look. "What about that night with—"

Allison cut her off. "We agreed you wouldn't bring that up ever again."

Molly smiled. "I'm just saying."

"Now go back out there and act like it was some lame joke or something. But you better be careful how you do it, because I think two of the Michelles take Tae Kwon Do."

"Really?"

"Yes. And one of them is the one who's twitching."

Molly turned off the faucets, unlocked the door, and walked back out. The sparse group had somehow taken the shape and demeanor of an angry mob. Molly made a point of keeping her distance from the Michelle with the twitch.

"Let me rephrase what I was saying," she offered. "It's perfect. You all did a wonderful job."

They traded some unsure looks, but then they smiled back at her.

"Go home. Get ready. Have a great time tonight."

She didn't have to tell them twice. Within moments, everyone was gone but Molly and Allison.

"That's good advice for you, too," Allison added. "Although you might consider taking a little nap first. You could use some beauty sleep."

"Sleep?" Molly laughed. "Who has time for sleep? That's what summer's for."

They walked to the door. Along the way, Molly was even able to overcome the urge to rearrange two nonsymmetrical centerpieces.

But just barely.

chapter TWO

Rachel wasn't sure if she'd rather be a journalist or a novelist, but she knew that she wanted to write. She loved everything about writing, from coming up with stories and creating characters to finding just the right word or turn of phrase. She liked the thought of working through the night under deadlines and pressure. And she especially liked how most writers seemed to have a smart-ass attitude.

She also liked the uniform, or rather, the lack of a uniform. Writers wore whatever they wanted, and that sounded great to Rachel. The thought of dressing up every day to go to work was practically suffocating. There were only two dresses in her closet—one for Easter and one for Christmas. On the other 363 days of the year, she was fully committed to jeans, shorts, and sweatpants.

That's why she felt so ridiculous standing on a platform in Matilda's Bridal and Formal Shop.

She was wearing a pink *peau de soie* dress with a pleated empire waist and tulle underskirt. The saleswoman assured her that these features were "perfect for your silhouette."

At the time, Rachel nodded like she understood what the woman was talking about. In truth, she was not only unfamiliar with the dress terms; she was completely unaware she even had a silhouette.

Yet, here she was wearing the dress, surrounded by mirrors— eight in all—and the image in each one was so absurd, she just had to laugh.

The more she looked, the more she laughed.

"No move," barked the tiny woman trying to perform the emergency alterations. Unlike the saleswoman who was all smiles and honey, the seamstress was packing major attitude. Rachel couldn't quite place the accent, maybe Eastern European, but her irritation transcended any linguistic boundaries.

"Too late, too late," the woman added for emphasis.

"I know," Rachel answered meekly. "I'm really sorry."

The seamstress scoffed and went back to work. Angry or not, she seemed to be doing a great job with the hem.

Rachel was only five four, and the dress was at least four inches too long. She was amazed at how fast the woman worked the pins from a cushion on her wrist into the dress.

She tried to make a mental picture so she could write about it later.

"You're really good," she said with a smile, trying to defuse the tension.

The woman looked up at her, and for a moment Rachel thought she might actually smile.

"Too late!"

Rachel just nodded and gave up on the notion of bonding with her. In truth, it really was too late for any alterations. The prom was now less than eight hours away.

If Rachel wanted to defend herself, and the woman gave no indication she was interested in such a discussion, she could have mentioned that her lateness wasn't a case of slacker procrastination or even bitchy perfectionism. Rachel hadn't come earlier because at no prior point did she ever imagine she'd be going to the prom.

It's not that she was one of those dark and brooding types who boycotted school functions on principle. She played French horn in the marching band and screamed her head off at football games. And, it wasn't because she was antisocial. She was cute, friendly, and loved to hang out.

Despite all of this, the high school social scene had been complicated for her. She had a lot of friends, but none who were very close. She never completely fit in with any one clique, so she bounced around from group to group.

When it came to boys, things had been even sketchier. She'd

been on a handful of dates, but something about them never felt quite right. She had fun, but she never had the range of emotions that she read about in books. (Or even on par with what she heard about in the girls' restroom.) After a particularly awkward New Year's Eve party, she came to the conclusion that she was probably gay.

This was not something she wanted to pursue over the last few months of high school. She suspected that when she got to college, there would be a world of discovery waiting for her. But, for the time being, she was content to avoid the dating scene altogether and concentrate on something that did come naturally—academics.

Unlike Molly, Rachel still had an Ivy League sticker on the back window of her car. In the fall, she'd be headed off to Dartmouth. There, on some cold New Hampshire night, she could finally explore her true sexuality.

Prom, she figured, was a casualty of the situation. Even if there was a girl she liked, she wasn't the type to make some big political statement and take her. (She wasn't even sure such a thing would be allowed.) Likewise, she didn't want to live out some lie by going with a boy.

When anyone asked if she was going, she just coyly answered, "I still haven't found the right person."

But a funny thing happened on the way to the closet. Earlier in the week, with absolutely no warning, Rachel was named to the prom court.

If this came as a surprise to the student body as a whole, it was a total shock to Rachel. At first she assumed that it was all a practical joke arranged by one of her friends on the school paper.

In fact, it had been her place on the newspaper staff that had put her in this position in the first place. Every month, Rachel wrote a "My Life as . . ." column. This was a first-person article about a different aspect of high school life. Her column was extremely humorous and the most popular feature in the paper. Two of her articles had caused minor firestorms.

"My Life as a Cafeteria Hag" detailed the inner workings of the school kitchen and included the actual ingredients of the weekly Sloppy Joes. As a result, the cafeteria manager was let go, and new sanitation standards had to be instituted.

Her most notorious column had featured an article about after-school jobs, in which she dressed like the furry mascot of a local ice-cream shop. The problem wasn't so much the content as its huge headline, which read, "My Life as a Giant Beaver." By the end of first period, she was already pleading her case to the principal that the headline did not mean what he thought it meant.

The final article in the series was supposed to be "My Life as a Prom Queen." To do it, Rachel had to submit her own name as a potential member of the prom court. Then, she was going to write humorously about what it was like to receive the fewest votes in the history of prom-queen balloting. At the conclusion of the article, she was going to skip out on prom and hang out with friends at an antiprom instead. This gave her not only a good ending, but also a nice cover for why she wasn't going.

But this plan was officially derailed when Mrs. White, the prom sponsor, assured her that it was no joke. She had honestly been elected as a member of the prom court.

The court was voted on by the entire senior class, and that had been the source of Rachel's surprising selection. The fact that she had never fully fit in with any one group helped her mostly fit in with every group. And, though she would never consider herself popular, she was exceedingly well-liked.

That afternoon, when Rachel was telling her mother the news, it dawned on her that as a member of the prom court, she should probably actually go to the prom. But for that she was lacking two key elements: a date and a dress.

That's when Mom came to the rescue.

Mrs. Buchanan, who was much hipper to her daughter's situation than Rachel realized, reassured her. "You don't really need a date," she explained. "It's not like going as a single is unprecedented."

"But dresses are expensive," Rachel responded. "And we're already on the hook for the tuition at Dartmouth, which is totally out of control. I can't believe I'm doing this to you."

"Yes, Rachel," her mother said in mock horror. "You were

accepted to an Ivy League school and got elected to prom court. How could you be so terrible to me?"

Rachel laughed. "You know what I mean. It just seems like a waste of money."

"The people have spoken," her mother replied with a smile. "And, they want you at the prom."

Rachel and her mother went dress shopping, and to her surprise, she actually enjoyed it. Dressing up every day was a pain, but on a special occasion it was all right. After a couple of shops they found Matilda's. There, in the window, Rachel saw the dress and fell for it even before the saleswoman gave her pitch.

When Rachel reached to check the price tag, her mom grabbed it out of her hand and simply said, "We'll take it."

Now, two days later, the final alterations were being done, and Rachel was looking at the dress in eight different mirrors. Her mother was off to the side, drinking a soda and trying just as hard as Rachel not to laugh at it all.

"No move," the seamstress said as she finished the hem and stepped back to check her work.

Rachel looked over at her mom, who had suddenly gone from laughing to teary eyed. Then she looked down at the seamstress.

"How do I look?" Rachel asked reflexively.

The little woman eyed her carefully, and suddenly Rachel wished she hadn't asked.

She looked Rachel in the eyes and with her broken accent

said, "You beauty." She paused for a moment and then added, "Late . . . but beauty." Finally, the woman smiled.

"That's bitchin'," Rachel said as her cheeks turned two shades of red. It was perhaps the greatest compliment she had ever heard.

chapter THREE

12:35 P.M.
7 hours and 25 minutes until prom

Kirby cringed when he heard the scream. Then a girl started to sob, and he used his big beefy hands to cover his ears. He was fearless on a football field. From the opening whistle to the final gun, he used his size and speed to dominate a game and terrorize the opposition. But ten minutes outside of a beauty parlor had turned him into a total basket case.

For the life of him, he could not imagine what was going on behind the blacked-out windows. Every instinct told him to use his size and speed to rush in and help whoever was doing the screaming and sobbing.

But he didn't.

He didn't because the same traits that made Kirby a great football player—that he was big and strong and did whatever he was told to do—also made him an ideal boyfriend.

His girlfriend, Jenna, told him that under no circumstance

could he come inside. She didn't even want him to wait for her, but on that point he insisted. It was prom day, and he wanted to spend as much time as possible with her. He'd be there the moment she got out.

It's not like Jenna had made up the ban. It was salon policy. There was a big sign on the door that read, NO MOMS! NO BOYS! NO WAY!

Normally the Rebecca Tyler Salon and Spa was much more welcoming of mothers and men. But this was no normal day. This was the one day each year when Rebecca closed her doors to everyone except for the girls of her alma mater. She had once been a cheerleader at Fletcher, and her school spirit still burned strong.

Inside, where boyfriends feared to tread, every chair and station was working at full capacity. The soothing new-age music had been replaced with a rowdy mix of rock, pop, and hip-hop. With no intruders, the girls were free to unload on any topic they wanted.

Conversations ran the gamut from the mundane to the raunchy. One group getting mani-pedis was trying to figure out a protocol for dancing with someone other than the guy who brought you. There was some disagreement about whether or not slow dances were off-limits.

Meanwhile, three girls with their hair up in curlers were playing a heated game of "Death Is Not an Option," in which two undesirable guys are listed and you have to decide which you'd be willing to hook up with.

The scream Kirby heard had come from a back room where a woman affectionately known as the "Dragon Lady of Death" was in charge of deep-tissue massage. The sobs were a natural by-product of hormones and insecurity mixed with way too much cappuccino. Add in gossip; sex talk; and the battling aromas of hair product, exfoliating wash, and body butter, and you had the perfect storm of teen anxiety.

Rebecca did everything she could to ease that anxiety. On one wall she'd hung an enlargement of her very own prom picture. In the photo, she sported big eighties hair and overly dramatic New Wave makeup. Underneath she had written, "Beauty is fleeting, but prom pictures last forever!"

She also wanted to make sure a lack of money didn't keep any of the girls from looking their best. So, she didn't charge them at all. She just asked that they tip the stylists and technicians as best as they could.

Her payment was simple. Every year, for weeks after the prom, she was visited by a steady stream of girls, each one dropping off a picture from the big night. Rebecca kept them in a set of photo albums that filled a shelf in her office.

"Think beautiful, be beautiful," she announced to no one in particular as she snaked her way through the crowd.

Two girls getting facial masks hardly needed the reminder. Unlike with Rachel, it had been a surprise to no one when Jenna and Victoria were named to prom court.

Jenna, whose boyfriend, Kirby, was still patiently waiting

outside, was a knockout. Tall and pretty, she looked like she belonged in a magazine. She lived in a small house with two younger sisters and her mother, who taught Spanish at the middle school. Despite the fact that they didn't have much money, Jenna had been voted Most Fashionable Girl in the senior class. This was a testament both to her sense of style and to her mother's excellent sewing skills.

At most schools, Jenna would have been *the* girl. But, at Fletcher, she resided in the heavy shadow of her best friend, Victoria Sligh.

Victoria was Fletcher's alpha girl, and she worked very hard to stay on top. Every August, a week before school started, she sat down with her mother and they wrote out an amazing list of type-A goals for the upcoming year. Invariably she achieved every one.

Behind her back, everyone (including Jenna) referred to her as Queen Victoria. And, though she never would have admitted it, she liked the nickname—a lot. She was an only child, and her parents (Dad was a surgeon, and Mom a former Miss Tennessee) pushed her to always keep striving for more.

"Try to relax," the woman said as she applied the mask to Victoria's face.

"I am relaxed," Victoria snapped back tartly.

"Of course," the woman said without missing a beat, skill-fully hiding any hint of sarcasm in her voice.

Jenna had to fight the urge to laugh out loud. She knew that her friend—who was wound pretty tightly on an average day—was particularly taut today.

Victoria was on the verge of completing the most ambitious of all her goals. It was a goal so ambitious she hadn't even written it down on her list for fear that someone might see it. She hadn't even told Jenna. She discussed it with only her mother.

Victoria was already the senior class president, homecoming queen, and captain of the cheerleading squad. If, as everyone expected, she took home the tiara as prom queen, she'd be the first girl in school history to win all four.

Her mother coined it "the Grand Slam."

It's hard to say which was more disturbing: the fact that Victoria actually went to the school library and looked through every old yearbook to find out if anyone else had accomplished the feat, or the fact that her mother thought it warranted a name. Either way, the two of them viewed it as the ultimate high school achievement.

But, hours away from her greatest triumph, Victoria was not feeling particularly triumphant. She had an uneasy feeling about the whole thing. She was worried that someone might ruin what she had worked so hard to accomplish.

Jenna sensed this and tried to be reassuring. "Don't worry," she said. "You're going to win."

Victoria despised being so transparent. She always wanted to project an image of total confidence, even with her best friend. "I don't know what you're talking about."

"You don't?" Jenna knew Victoria better than anyone. They had been best friends since back in middle school, when Victoria was still just Vicki.

"No," replied Victoria. "I don't."

"What I'm talking about is your raging case of *Venus envy*," Jenna said. (Now it was the woman applying the mask who had to fight the urge to laugh.)

"My *what* envy?"

"*Venus* envy. It's when one hot girl is jealous of another hot girl," Jenna explained.

Victoria sat upright, her face mostly covered with a green mask, but her look of contempt plainly visible. "You think I'm jealous? Of whom?"

The *whom* cracked Jenna up. It was so AP English of Victoria.

Jenna sat up and slyly nodded at the girl directly in front of them getting a sea-salt scrub. "You're jealous of Karolina Olsen."

Victoria was busted, but she wasn't going to give in. "I'm not jealous of her," she protested.

Jenna smiled. "But you are worried about her."

That was an understatement. Victoria and her mother had talked it over and decided that Karolina was the one girl who could pull the prom queen upset. It was a development they hadn't seen coming at the start of the year when they first mapped out the Grand Slam plan.

Karolina arrived suddenly and unexpectedly on the first day of school. Normally, a new girl couldn't disrupt the power structure too much. But Karolina wasn't a typical new girl.

She was a Swedish exchange student.

She was flawlessly beautiful and disgustingly sweet, and she exuded an innocent sexiness that had most boys at school wrapped around her finger.

The fact that Karolina was so comfortable lying half-naked in a roomful of strangers was just one of the many things about her that unnerved Victoria. She was just so . . . European.

Victoria was pretty, but she had to work at it. She kept to a strict diet, worked out religiously, and always made sure her hair and makeup were perfect. All that work gave her a certain hardness.

Karolina was just naturally beautiful. She could goof around with the guys, eat a ton of pizza, and none of it had the slightest impact.

Karolina also had a secret weapon—actually, two of them—a pair of breasts that were so impressive, they had their own nickname: the Olsen Twins.

This was a sensitive issue with Victoria and her mother, both of whom were borderline B cups at best. (Victoria's mom claimed her lack of success at the Miss America pageant had to do with the fact that as Miss Tennessee, she always had to stand next to Miss Texas, a girl from Dallas whose fake boobs made Victoria's mom look even more flat chested by comparison.)

In a close election, Karolina's breasts could be worth maybe fifty votes. And that's what was worrying Victoria. She didn't want to be the prom queen. She *needed* it. And she didn't like leaving anything to chance.

"It's not whatever you called it," Victoria said.

"Venus envy?"

"Right. It's not that."

"Then what is it?" Jenna asked.

Victoria hesitated for a moment and then said out loud what she had been thinking all week. "It's completely unfair that she's on the prom court."

"I knew it. I knew it," Jenna said, laughing. "Why do you think it's unfair?"

"She's an *exchange* student," Victoria reasoned. "She should be the Ice Princess of Stockholm or something like that. But she shouldn't be *our* prom queen. She doesn't represent who we are."

"Wow," Jenna said, realizing this meant even more to Victoria than she had thought. "It's not like the prom queen's a member of Congress. It's just some girl who poses for a picture."

This last dig cut deep. "Well, she shouldn't be the one posing," Victoria said. "It should be me."

"Thanks a lot," Jenna said pointedly. "I guess I don't represent who we are either."

"Or you," Victoria added with a cringe. She was so focused on Karolina that she forgot her best friend was also still technically in the running. "It just shouldn't be her."

They sat there for a moment watching as Karolina continued her sea-salt scrub, completely oblivious to the rage of emotions brewing around her.

Jenna knew that Victoria rubbed a lot of people the wrong way. But their friendship went back a long way and that meant a lot. They had been through so much together, and Jenna knew that her friend had a lot of really great qualities. Still, she enjoyed poking her every now and then.

"Look at her," Jenna said, motioning back to Karolina. "Tell me that you're not jealous at least a little bit."

"Not a bit," Victoria said unconvincingly.

Just then, Karolina turned over slightly, exposing one of the Olsen Twins. The two of them were momentarily speechless.

"Which one is that?" Jenna asked with a smile. "Mary-Kate or Ashley?"

chapter FOUR

3:46 P.M.
4 hours and 14 minutes until prom

All the presets on the radio in Matt Hall's truck were set to country music stations. An active member of the Fellowship of Christian Athletes, he was seriously considering becoming a youth minister. But his favorite song—the one that literally brought tears to his eyes—was not some twangy country ballad or even a moving gospel hymn. It was an old eighties hit sung by an effeminate man partial to eyeliner, paisley coats, frilly ruffles, and high-heeled boots.

You couldn't actually call Matt a Prince fan; he only liked a few of Prince's songs. But "Purple Rain" quite simply rocked his world. It could not play without him lip-synching every word and playing air guitar along with each note.

The reason had everything to do with Matt being the best athlete at Fletcher High School. Matt had been on one team or another every day he was in high school. Whenever he and the rest of the Fletcher Senators took the field, they did so in purple-and-white uniforms. And whenever they left the field victorious, they celebrated by blasting "Purple Rain" full volume on an old boom box.

It was a tradition that Matt held dear.

A three-sport letterman, he was the unquestioned leader of the football, basketball, and baseball teams. He was also pretty nice and down to earth. Guys wanted to be his friend, and girls wanted to be something more.

But that role was taken by Queen Victoria.

Matt and Victoria officially started dating on Valentine's Day of their junior year. This, like almost everything else about their lives, seemed just a little too perfect.

In truth, Victoria had been angling to hook up with him long before that. She had her eye on Matt all through sophomore year, when he was dating a senior. (Victoria was popular, but she couldn't compete with a senior who was also popular.) Instead, she waited, assuming the relationship would end when his girlfriend left for college.

Throughout the first semester of their junior year, she made a point of hanging out with Matt strictly as a friend. All the while, she waited for the inevitable breakup of his long-distance relationship. That happened over Christmas vacation, and when Victoria got the word, she dumped her boyfriend on the spot.

The next day Victoria and Matt began consoling each

other about their respective broken hearts. (His real, hers self-inflicted.)

He didn't stand a chance.

"I never imagined this would happen," she told him one tearful night a few weeks later. "But I don't think I can go on just being your friend."

It was beyond lame. But Matt, being a guy, bought it all the way.

A lot of girls seriously doubted she cared about him. They figured he was just another one of the goals on her checklist. He was, after all, the school's top catch, and she would settle for nothing less. But now, more than a year later, it was hard to imagine them any way but together.

Still, they weren't a perfect match. She cared about appearances and he didn't. (She didn't talk to him for a week after he and the rest of the football team got Mohawks as a sign of team spirit.) She also refused to ride in his beat-up truck, which he refused to turn in for something newer. (His family had the money; he just didn't see the point.)

Their biggest difference, though, was in the way they viewed competition. Both of them were extremely competitive, but in very different ways. Victoria wanted to win because she wanted to be the best. Matt loved to compete as part of a team. He didn't care one bit about personal awards. He wanted the team to come together and win.

That's why, at the same time Victoria was stressing about

whether she would beat Karolina, Matt was focused on how to help a teammate. Matt was the catcher on the school's baseball team, which at the moment was locked in a battle with its rival school—West High.

Prom was supposed to take place on a day with no other school activities. But a rainout had forced the game to be rescheduled, and to the delight of the players, this was the only day both schools could make it. It gave them the perfect excuse to be away from the massive prama unfolding back home.

Once they got home after the game, there'd be enough time for only a quick shower before rushing off to dinner. Some even joked that if they got lucky, the game might go into extra innings. That way they could miss most of the dance, too.

But Matt didn't want any extra innings. He just wanted to win the game so that he could listen to his favorite song on the bus ride home.

Fletcher had a one-run lead and was an out away from winning. But there was a runner on third base and the pitcher seemed to be losing his cool. That's why Matt called a time-out and walked the ball back to the mound.

The pitcher was anxious and was expecting Matt to tell him to calm down. Then they could talk over the batter and agree on a pitch. But Matt had a different approach.

He handed him the ball and gave him a long look before asking, "What are you doing tonight after the prom?"

The pitcher wasn't exactly sure where this was going.

Matt just kept talking. "Victoria had me get a suite over at the Hilton for an after-party. It's got a couple of rooms and a big plasma TV. It's really nice."

"What are you talking about?"

"I'm just saying," Matt continued, "that if you and your girl-friend want to come over, you're more than welcome. What do you think?"

"We're kind of in the middle of something," he said.

"You mean you guys already had plans for afterward?"

"No," the pitcher said, dumbfounded. "I mean we're in the middle of a baseball game."

"Well, actually, we're not," Matt replied. "We're at the end of a baseball game. And, actually, this one's already over."

"How's that?"

And this is what made Matt special to his teammates. He always knew just what to say. "There's no way this guy can handle the pressure or hit your stuff. He's going to swing at the first pitch—a low slider by the way—and hit some weak-ass grounder. This game is over."

The talk had the desired effect as the pitcher laughed and relaxed considerably. "I guess you got everything figured out."

"Well, not everything," Matt said. "I still need to figure out this party. I mean, the after-party is just as important as the prom. At least that's what Victoria says. I honestly don't know why that is. It would seem to me that the prom was much more important, but I'm just a dumb jock. Now are you guys coming or not?"

"Get behind the plate," the pitcher said, motioning toward home.

Matt could tell by his expression that he was ready. He walked back to the plate and squatted down into position. "I hope your girlfriend's not here," he said, looking up at the batter. "Because you are about to make a horse's ass of yourself."

The batter gulped and Matt knew it was over. The pitch came in and he swung at it. It was a weak grounder, just like he said. But it was a little too weak. It was slow enough that the runner from third was almost home when the pitcher fielded the ball and threw it to Matt.

The runner's only chance was to crash into Matt as hard as possible to knock the ball loose. They had a massive collision, and Matt slammed into the ground, hitting his head against home plate. There was a hush as the umpire looked down to see if he was still holding the ball.

When the umpire called, "Out," Matt's teammates went wild and started piling up on him. Despite the crushing weight of the other players and the pain from the collision, Matt was in heaven.

In his heart of hearts, he knew that he was too small to play college football or basketball. He might be able to make the baseball team at a medium-sized school, but his moments of sports glory were numbered. He needed to savor them while he could.

Twenty minutes later Matt was holding an ice pack to the side of his head as the team bus rumbled down the highway. The pitcher came up and sat down in the seat in front of him.

"Is that ice for the collision or the celebration?" he asked.

"I think it's a little bit of both," Matt said.

He moved the pack and revealed a dark bruise under his eye from where the catcher's mask had slammed into his cheek.

"That's going to leave a mark," the pitcher said, cringing.

"Hurts like a bitch," Matt said.

"I got to hand it to you. It happened just like you said it would."

"Really, because I don't remember telling you I'd get hit by a truck at home plate," Matt joked. "I figured you would throw it to first for the force out."

The pitcher thought for a moment. "I guess that would have been the smarter play. Next time, you should be more specific."

They both laughed.

"Just think," the pitcher added, "you'll remember that play every time you look at your prom picture, because you'll have a big bad black eye."

Suddenly, Matt's smile disappeared. He had forgotten about the pictures. He knew that they were a big deal to Victoria.

"I didn't think about that," he said, trying to look at his reflection in the bus window. "Victoria wouldn't talk to me when I got a Mohawk. I wonder how she'll handle this."

"What would she rather have?" the pitcher asked. "Pretty pictures, or a boyfriend who made a game-saving play?"

"Are you kidding?" Matt laughed. "She couldn't care less about the game." He thought about it for a moment and knew what he said was true. She didn't care about whether the team won or not. But he cared.

Before he could worry about it too much, a finger pushed the play button on an ancient boom box. The music began, and Prince started playing the guitar.

"Excuse me," Matt said to his friend, his smile returning. "They're playing my song.

"I never meant to cause you any sorrow," he sang off-key at the top of his lungs, loving every second of it. *"I never meant to cause you any pain."*

chapter **FIVE**

1:07 p.m.
6 hours and 53 minutes until prom

As her near meltdown in front of the prom committee suggested, Molly had more than a few obsessive-compulsive traits. Whether she was arranging her bookshelves alphabetically by author or making playlists for her iPod that were precisely forty-five minutes long (she listened to them while she rode an exercise bike), she liked things organized and according to schedule.

For her birthday, her best friend, Allison, had given her the *Too Hot to Handle* calendar, which had pictures of hunky firemen wearing just enough gear to be appropriate. Within an hour, she'd already marked the key dates for her friends' birthdays, AP and SAT test dates, and, of course, graduation. She would have done it faster, except she was having a birthday party at the time.

The first thing she marked on the calendar, though, was

the date for prom, on which she simply wrote, "P-Day." At the time it seemed so far away. Now she couldn't believe that it had finally arrived.

When she got home from the American Legion hall, she found her mother in the kitchen, singing along with some song she didn't recognize.

"What's this?" she asked.

"Duran Duran," her mother said. When she turned around, Molly saw she was wearing a T-shirt that had "Prom Mom" written on it.

"Why are you wearing that?" Molly moaned.

Mrs. Walker smiled. "Because my daughter gave it to me."

"Technically the prom committee gave it to you," Molly explained. "I was against it from the beginning."

"Either way, it was a gift. So I'm going to cherish it."

Molly saw some old yearbooks lying out on the kitchen table. "Old-people yearbooks. Old-people music. What's going on?"

"Helping you guys yesterday got me thinking about my prom," she explained. "So I dusted these off to flip through them."

Molly looked down at one of the yearbooks. Her mother's prom picture had been stuck between the pages. She looked at it for a moment and tried to imagine what her mother would have been like at seventeen.

"So, who is this guy?" Molly asked, pointing at the picture.

"Forrest Boone," her mother answered.

"Forrest Boone? Sounds like an air freshener."

"Well, I thought he was just dreamy. He played football, and he told me that I was the only girl he ever loved."

Suddenly, Molly got interested. "And . . ."

Mom smiled. "I wasn't even the only girl he loved on prom night."

"Ouch. That must have been awful."

"You'd think so. But it wasn't, really. I had built that night up so much that he couldn't possibly have lived up to my imagination. He ended up leaving without me, and I had a lot more fun after he was gone. I danced with some other boys, including your father."

"And that's when you two fell in love," Molly added.

"No," her mother laughed. "You watch too many movies. But that's when I realized being happy was much more important than being with Mr. Dreamboat."

"Whatever happened to Forrest Boone?"

"I'm happy to report that he is fat, balding, and a mediocre accountant."

"Things work out," Molly said.

"With a vengeance."

Molly's mother picked up her purse off the counter.

"I've got to run some errands. You want to grab some lunch?"

"I can't," Molly told her. "I've got a schedule to keep."

Mrs. Walker had heard that many times. "Have fun," she said as she headed out the door. "Feel free to keep listening to this good music."

Molly rolled her eyes. "I think I'll opt for this century."

Molly checked the clock and realized she had a little bit of time before she had to be somewhere. She gave herself exactly seventeen minutes for a power nap.

Three hours later, her mother came home with an armful of groceries and found Molly still sprawled across the couch in a sleep so deep she didn't even notice the dog licking her face. So far, Molly had slept through lunch (no big deal), a trip to the florist (medium-sized deal), and her hair appointment (very big deal).

Mrs. Walker shooed away the dog and cringed. She didn't know how long Molly had been asleep, but she was pretty certain the scene was about to turn ugly.

"Molly," she said in a voice that was sweet but firm. "Time to wake up."

Molly didn't move a muscle. She just lay there like the victims in those crime-scene shows she liked so much.

This time her mother reached down and shook her by the shoulder. "Molly, you've got to wake up."

There was still no response.

Finally, Mom resorted to the fail-safe option. "Molly, it's time for prom."

There it was—the four-letter word guaranteed to wake her out of any sleep. Molly bolted upright, looked around the room for a moment, and panicked.

"Ohmigod," she blurted as she tried to get her bearings. "What time is it?"

Her mother hesitated, knowing she wouldn't like the answer. "Four."

"Ohmigod!" Now she was about to hyperventilate. She ran through her schedule in her head. "Hair. Florist. Dress. He's going to be here any minute."

"Calm down," Mrs. Walker said. "He's not going to be here any minute. He's going to be here in an hour and a half. You've got plenty of time."

"Plenty of time," Molly exclaimed. She pointed at her hair. The humidity-fueled frizz had now been accented with three hours of bed head. "Have you seen this?"

Mrs. Walker gave her a quick look and a smile. "Every day, when I look in the mirror."

Molly's hair had definitely come to her by way of her mother's DNA. Luckily, that meant Mom knew all the tricks of the trade. She may not have been the Rebecca Tyler Salon and Spa, but she was more than up to the challenge. She could make sure her hair was perfect. Molly's state of mind, however, was a completely different subject.

Molly had been in a major funk all week. Despite her nearly clinical obsession with detail, she had made it to prom day minus one very important one—a boyfriend.

She'd had a boyfriend as recently as six days earlier. But the relationship had been a victim of the prom itself. (Allison called it a "first-degree promicide.")

Molly had been dating Cameron for about three and a half

months. Both of them had big plans for the big night. Molly wanted it to be the perfect high school conclusion—a party for the ages. "Good music, good friends, good times," she liked to say.

Cameron was far more interested in what was going to happen afterward. He thought it was the perfect time to take that final step in their relationship. He assumed she'd be thrilled when he told her that he'd gotten a hotel room.

She wasn't.

It wasn't just that she was unsure about having sex with Cam. (She was actually fifty-fifty on the topic.) It was the bold manner in which he just went ahead and got the room without talking to her about it. It never dawned on him that she wouldn't automatically jump at the chance to cap off prom night by surrendering her virginity down at the Ramada.

Her less-than-enthusiastic reaction led to an epic argument in which he had the nerve to complain that he'd already put down a nonrefundable deposit. It ended with both of them storming off to cool down.

The following morning she found him waiting by her locker. She thought he was there to apologize. Then she noticed he was holding a sweater she'd left over at his house. He was there to break up. He gave her the "We can still be friends" talk.

The freaking nerve.

As if she'd want to remain friends with a guy who was dumping her the week of prom.

Molly cried all through first and second periods and then bombed an English test that she had completely studied for. Over the week, sadness turned to frustration and then into full-blown anger. She was furious at him. But she was also angry at herself.

What if she'd been the problem? Maybe it was time for *that* night. Maybe she was so obsessed with planning the perfect night that she ruined what could have been . . . the perfect night.

After all of her hard work, there was no way she wasn't going to go. And, unlike her friend Rachel, there was no way she was going single. If she was by herself, everyone would ask where Cam was, and she'd spend her whole damn night getting depressed over and over again.

That was completely unacceptable.

She decided she had to make a show of strength.

Unfortunately, there were not a lot of real desirable guys still on the market in the last days before the dance. Fletcher had been pretty much mined out. That meant she had to look to other schools, which is where she found Ben.

Technically, Aunt Linda found Ben. She lived about forty-five minutes away and said the boy next door would be perfect. Desperate, Molly jumped at the opportunity, sight unseen. Now, she was worried that she'd made another big mistake.

On the night of her "Hollywood Dreams," she wanted to be Audrey Hepburn. But what if her date turned out to be Alfred Hitchcock.

She looked in the mirror as her mom was working some more product into her hair. "I'm pathetic," she said matter-of-factly.

"Because your mother's doing your hair?"

"Well, that, too," Molly said with a laugh. "But that's not what I meant."

"Then what makes you pathetic?"

"Everything," Molly said. "It's bad enough that I'm taking a safety choice for college. Was it too much to ask not to go with one to prom?"

"First of all," her mother said, "just because it isn't Princeton, doesn't mean it's a safety school. And, secondly, from what Linda tells me, this boy's got a lot going for him."

"He mows her lawn," Molly said, rolling her eyes. "What does he have going for him? That he's good with a Weed Eater?"

"She said that he was cute, smart, and funny."

Molly gave her a skeptical look. "We're trusting the judgment of a woman who once thought Uncle Harold was cute, smart, and funny."

Mrs. Walker had to concede this point. "True. But, I have impeccable taste. And he sounded cute when I talked to him on the phone."

Molly pulled away and turned to her mother.

"When you *what*?" she demanded.

Her mother cringed and waited a moment before answering. "When I talked to him on the phone. He called me today."

Molly couldn't believe it. "He called *you*?"

"Yes. He had some questions."

Now Molly was up from her seat, with her hands on her hips. This was the "frustrated" pose she had long ago perfected. "What kinds of questions?" she wanted to know.

Mrs. Walker hemmed and hawed for a moment. "I'm not supposed to tell you."

"What? Is there some parent–psycho stalker confidentiality I don't know about?"

"It wasn't psychotic," her mother said. "It was cute."

"I can't believe this," Molly complained. "My life just keeps getting worse."

Now Mom gave her a look. "He just wanted to know the prom's theme and the color of your dress."

This caught Molly off guard, and she lowered her hands from her hips a little bit. In nearly four months of dating, she couldn't imagine Cameron even realizing the prom had a theme.

"Why?" she asked, her tone softening.

"He wanted to make sure he got the right tux and corsage," she explained.

Now, Molly really had no idea what to think. "I guess that is kind of cute," she said, a small smile forming.

"I thought so," her mother replied.

chapter SIX

Ben was hard to miss as he hurried through the mall. He was tall, over six foot two, and took long, loping strides. Each one was punctuated by the loud slap of his flip-flops. He had a shaggy mop of hair that bounced up and down as he ran and a big goofy smile that somehow made the whole image irresistible.

Aunt Linda had been right on the money. Ben was definitely cute. He was also lost, which is why he was running around looking for a map, a security guard, or anyone who could point him in the direction of Frankie's Formal Wear.

In all the times he'd been to the mall, he'd never noticed the tuxedo shop. Then again, in all those times he'd never needed a tux. Normally, he wasn't interested in going anywhere you couldn't go wearing a T-shirt and board shorts.

But for a blind date with Molly, he was willing to make an exception.

Technically, Ben did not consider it a blind date. He preferred to think of it as visually impaired, because he had a decent idea of what she looked like. Even though she didn't realize it, they'd met before, and for him it had been memorable. Unfortunately, they were both thirteen at the time.

It was between seventh and eighth grades, and Ben was spending the summer with his grandparents, who lived next door to Molly's aunt and uncle. One day, when Molly was visiting her cousins, both families went out for ice cream.

Later, he told his buddies back home in Boston that he'd gone out for ice cream with a girl who was "wicked hot." Of course, he left out the part about being too nervous to say a single word to her. Five years later, he was getting a second chance to "close the deal," as he and his buddies like to joke.

This was perfect for Ben because his greatest strength had always been his ability to put a strong finish on a mediocre start. It was true in the classroom, where midterm C's and B-minuses invariably became B-pluses and A's. And, it was true in the swimming pool, where he'd be in the middle of the pack for most of a race only to touch the wall ahead of everybody else.

Now, he was hoping that it would be true of high school.

His senior year could certainly use a strong finish to make

up for its start. It began with Ben's parents getting divorced over the summer. He was devastated, first when they split and then when he and his mother had to leave Boston and move in with his grandparents.

On his first day at West High, the only seniors he knew were senior citizens. He was not much fun to be around. But, after a couple of months of gloom and doom, two of his favorite things helped ease Ben's transition into his new school—swimming and television.

He had been a top swimmer at his old school and was an instant hit with his new teammates. He helped West win its first district championship in years, and he made some good friends in the process. Despite his athletic success, most people at school didn't know him as a swimmer. (After all, how many people actually go to a swim meet?) They knew him as a schoolwide television personality.

Every day Ben's television production class produced a five-minute broadcast for the school. During the first semester, he worked behind the scenes, operating a camera or directing the show. But after winter break everyone switched positions, and he was assigned to be on camera. He was responsible for the "Thought for the Day."

He was hilarious, which is not something the "Thought for the Day" had traditionally been.

The girl who'd had the job before him had taken it way too seriously for his taste. Each day she read some deeply moving inspirational piece that put everyone to sleep. He decided to liven it up by doing each day's thought in character.

Sometimes the thoughts were brief and to the point, like when he dressed as a surfer and told everyone, "Don't be rude. Be a dude." Other thoughts were friendly reminders, like when Conan the Librarian warned, "Turn in your overdue books or I will beat you into pulp fiction." The most popular character was Hippie Hank, who dressed in sixties psychedelic clothes and ended all of his thoughts with the catch phrase, "Remember that love is always the answer . . . unless the question is multiple choice. Then, the answer is B."

Despite making a lot of new friends and finally fitting in at school, Ben never had a girlfriend at West. The front-row seat for his parents' divorce had soured him on relationships. He knew that inevitably there would be a breakup and it would be messy.

There were a couple of girls he went out with (and a few more that he made out with) but none who became steady dates. This wasn't just because of his parents. He didn't want to get too serious, with college coming up in the fall. (He had his fingers crossed that a spot on the waiting list at Northwestern would turn into a yes.) The last thing he needed was a girl making him feel guilty about going away to school.

Still, when Aunt Linda asked if he'd be interested in taking Molly to the prom, he said yes right away. It was the perfect situation because it was a one-night deal. He could be dashing, romantic, and all those things he hadn't been with the girls at West. Then when it was over, he could go home.

At least, that's what he told himself. There was a part of him that imagined it might be some kind of fated thing. He'd never admit this, but it was the only explanation for how excited he was. Cool, detached guys don't run frantically around the mall in search of Frankie's Formal Wear.

A guy behind the counter greeted him with a cheesy line: "Welcome to Frankie's, where you don't need bucks to get a good tux."

"My name's Ben Bauer," he said breathlessly. "We talked on the phone."

"Oh, yes," the counterman replied. "The really tall kid, who needed a tux really fast."

"You said you can help me," Ben reminded him hopefully.

The guy smiled. "I'm sure we can fix you up."

"The prom theme is California Dreaming," Ben offered.

"The theme—" the man started to say.

"No, wait," Ben interrupted. He dug into his pocket and pulled out a crumpled piece of paper and looked at it. "I mean Hollywood Dreams."

The guy waited a moment to make sure Ben was really done this time. "What I was going to say is that the theme is not usually a factor in what you wear. It's more of a decoration thing. This is especially true for the guys. A tux is a tux."

"Are you sure?" This was Ben's first prom.

"I work in the tuxedo industry," he said. "It's kind of my thing to know. Let's get you measured."

While he was getting measured, Ben noticed an ad for the shop. It had a picture of Humphrey Bogart in *Casablanca*. In the picture, he was wearing a black bow tie and a white dinner jacket. It screamed cool.

"That's it," Ben said, pointing at the picture. "'Hollywood Dreams.'"

The guy looked at the picture and nodded. "Good call. I think we have a white dinner jacket in back."

Ben didn't bother with a tux bag; he just wore it out of the store. If he looked out of place before, he looked even more so now as he hurried over to the florist shop.

The young woman behind the counter instantly recognized the situation. "Looks like someone's rushing off to prom," she said with just a hint of flirt in her voice.

"Yes," he said. "And I need a corsage that goes with a dress that is antique rose and dusty white."

She gave him a sideways glance. "Do you maybe mean *dusty* rose with *antique* white?"

He reached into his pocket and pulled out the crumpled paper again. "Yes," he answered, a bit flustered. "What you just said. Do you have one?"

"Of course," she smiled. "Do you want a wristlet or a pin-on?"

Ben's eyes opened wide. "A what or a what?"

"A wristlet or a pin-on," she said. "A wristlet is a corsage she would wear around her wrist like this." She demonstrated. "A pin-on is a corsage that you would pin to her dress."

Ben had a pained expression as he tried to figure out an answer. He didn't know which way to go. "I'll take both," he said, reaching for his wallet.

"We have dozens to choose from," she said.

"Dozens?" Ben asked. "I couldn't choose between the wristlet and pin-on. How am I going to choose between dozens?"

She thought for a moment. "Do you know what her favorite type of flower is?"

He shook his head. "I know she likes rocky road ice cream," he said, remembering their first meeting. "Or at least she did when she was thirteen."

The salesclerk had no idea what ice cream had to do with it, but she played along. "Well, most girls like roses."

He smiled. "Roses sound good," he said. "And her dress has that rose color in it."

"Dusty rose," she offered.

"Right. Dusty rose. Let's go with roses."

"Good idea," she said, nodding. "That narrows it some. Now, what are you trying to say with the corsage."

He gave her a blank look. This was much more complicated than he ever imagined.

"Are you looking for an 'I think you're special' corsage? A 'We're just friends' corsage? Or something in the 'I love you' vein?"

He thought long and hard. He knew this was important. "Do you have anything in a 'Dare to be great'?"

She thought for a moment and smiled. "I think so."

Moments later, Ben was rushing through the parking lot in a tuxedo carrying not one but two corsages—a wristlet and a pin-on. When he got to the car, he placed them on the passenger seat, making sure the containers were directly in line with the air-conditioner vent. He didn't think it would make for a good introduction to arrive with wilted flowers.

As he went to get in the car, he had another thought. He didn't think it would be a good idea to arrive with a wilted tux either. He took off the jacket and the shirt and hung them in the backseat.

Now he looked utterly ridiculous. He had on dress shoes, tuxedo pants, and the old Boston Red Sox shirt he'd been wearing when he arrived.

His mind raced in every direction during the car ride. He practiced a whole series of introductions.

"Hello, my name is Ben," he tried with a deep voice.

"Hi, I'm Ben," he said, trying to sound more friendly.

He even practiced a string of compliments.

"That's a lovely dress."

"Nice dress."

"Damn, that dress is *fine*."

None of them sounded particularly effective.

By the time he started doing the lines as Hippie Hank and

Conan the Librarian, he knew that he was in trouble. Finally, he looked at himself in the rearview mirror. "You are such a freaking goofball."

He pulled up to Molly's house two minutes early. That gave him just enough time to take a deep breath and change back into his tux. Of course the only place he had to change was right out on the street. (After years of swim meets he was pretty used to stripping down in public, although he hadn't figured that she would be looking out her bedroom window at him.)

"He's here," Molly called out to her mother.

"How does he look?" Mom asked, getting straight to the point.

"Explain this one for me," she called out. "He's wearing tuxedo pants and a Boston Red Sox T-shirt."

"Is it maybe some new fashion?" Mrs. Walker said as she came into the room and looked out with her daughter.

"Not on this planet," Molly said.

Then he took off his shirt to reveal a rather well-defined body. Years of swimming had done their job.

"Well, well," Molly said with a slight gasp. "I see why Aunt Linda likes him to mow her lawn."

Mom just nodded.

Next he put on his shirt and jacket.

"Definitely cute," Molly admitted when he was done. "At least the pictures will look good."

"There's more to life than pictures," her mom reminded her.

"You mean like sex and alcohol," Molly joked.

"You're killing me," her mother said.

There was a knock on the front door, and Mrs. Walker went to answer it while Molly waited in the room. She wasn't going to look too eager.

From down the hall she could hear the sounds of Ben coming inside and talking to her mom. Finally, she couldn't wait any longer. She went out to the hall.

Ben looked at her. She had grown up exactly as he had imagined. "Hi, I'm Ben," he said, flashing a smile.

"I'm Molly."

There was a momentary pause before he added, "Wow, that's a really great dress." This was not one of the practiced lines. This was an unavoidable truth.

Molly smiled and gave a quick look to her mom. "Thank you."

He snapped out of his momentary stare and remembered the corsages. "I don't know if you realize this," he said, his voice cracking a bit, "but there are actually two types of corsages. I went ahead and got you both so you could pick what you liked better."

He showed them to her. They were beautiful.

"They're both lovely," Molly said. Now her voice was cracking.

"Would you like the pin-on?" he asked.

"Sure," she said awkwardly.

He held up the corsage and went to pin it, but he hesitated.

He reached into his pocket and pulled out another crumpled sheet of paper.

"The woman at the florist shop gave me this in case you picked the pin-on," he explained.

He turned away slightly to read the directions. "Hold the corsage by the stem and place it on the lapel at the collarbone," he said to himself, twisting his hand into the right position.

"You know," Molly said, coming to the rescue, "the wristlet will be fine."

Ben breathed a sigh of relief.

"Great," he said. "I don't even need directions for that one."

He put the wristlet on her arm, and for the first time they touched. It was just a finger on the wrist, but he liked it. They both did. When he was done, he turned to Molly's mother.

"Mrs. Walker," he said gallantly. "These are for you."

He handed her the extra corsage and she laughed. She couldn't help it. "Thank you," she said, unsure what she was supposed to do with it.

Another pause in the conversation.

"Oh, there is one problem," he said. "About the car."

Originally Molly and Cameron were going to go with two other couples and Cameron was responsible for getting the limo. But since there was no Cameron, there was no limo. Even if Molly's Volvo was big enough to hold six, there's no way they could rely on it. So Ben had volunteered to provide the wheels.

"What's the problem?" Molly asked slightly worried.

"I couldn't find anything cool," he explained. "The only car I could get big enough to hold six people is my grandpa's Lincoln Continental. It's kind of ugly and it smells like old people."

Molly looked out the window at the car. Earlier, she had been too focused on looking at Ben to notice.

"That's right," Ben said. "Instead of a limo, I brought you a lame-o."

Molly laughed and when she did, she smiled.

It was the same smile that he had remembered for the last five years.

chapter SEVEN

5:41 P.M.
2 hours and 19 minutes until prom

Karolina looked out the window and laughed. During her year in the States, she found the defining trait of most Americans was that they were impressed by things that were large. Houses looked like mansions. Restaurants served giant portions. And, as she was well aware, boys paid attention to girls with big boobs.

Now she was looking out of the window of her host family's house at a limousine that stretched the length of at least three normal cars. It was absurd, she thought. She would have to take a picture because her friends back home in Sweden would never believe it.

Karolina was excited about going to the prom. But, unlike most of the girls, who were looking for some version of romance, she was going strictly for research.

Everyone talked about prom like it was the most important

night of their lives. At her high school back in Stockholm, there was a formal dance called the *studentballen* held the week before graduation. It was nice, but it wasn't a life-or-death event. There was no king or queen and certainly no stretch limousines. She was dying to see firsthand what this night was really like.

In fact, prom was a prime example of why Karolina loved her year as an exchange student. Just reading about it wouldn't do. She could study English and American history back home, but some things just had to be experienced.

In biology class she'd seen a documentary about Jane Goodall going to Africa to study chimpanzees by living with them. She felt like the Jane Goodall of American teenagers. Instead of learning how a chimp used a twig to make a tool, she learned how a girl used a boy to make another boy jealous.

Before coming to the United States, most of what she knew about high school life in America came from countless viewings of her favorite movie—*Grease*. She learned English by watching the DVD over and over again. But, while it helped linguistically, the students at Rydell were very different from the ones at Fletcher.

When she arrived, the first thing she noticed was how all the kids split up into the different cliques. At first, in part because of her looks and in part because she was new and a little exotic, she got sucked into the popular crowd. This was Victoria's group, and Karolina was amazed at how catty all the girls were. It's not like there weren't bitchy girls back in Sweden. It's just that here those girls seemed to dominate the school.

During the first couple of weeks, Victoria even acted like she wanted to be friends. One time the two of them went clothes shopping together. More than anything, Karolina went along to see a mall up close with an obvious expert. But she was instantly turned off by how mean-spirited Victoria could be. She talked about everyone behind his or her back, even her best friend.

"I'm so glad Jenna couldn't make it," Victoria had confided in Karolina that day. "I love her to death, but it's such a drag to shop with her because she can't afford anything. It makes you feel guilty whenever you buy something."

Karolina couldn't believe it. The next day at lunch, she actually had the nerve to turn Victoria down when the queen motioned for her to come sit at her table. Things had been frosty between them ever since.

Despite her appearance, Karolina had a serious geek streak. She fit in much better with the kids who were academic but not particularly cool. She'd actually become tight with Molly and Allison and could never imagine either of them speaking about a friend the way Victoria had.

Among the uncool aspects of high school life that Karolina embraced was school spirit. There was nothing like it at her *gymnasieskol* back in Sweden. There, you went to class and went home. Now, she always wore purple on the days of big games, and she got involved in a variety of after-school clubs and activities.

She joined Interact and student government, which had their share of popular kids. But she also got involved in traditional loser groups like the international and chess clubs. (As a result, attendance at chess club meetings set all-time records.)

It was in chess club that Karolina first met her prom date. Chas Montgomery was not a likely choice to escort anyone to the prom, much less a member of the prom court. Over the years Chas had battled the three A's of teen pain—acne, asthma, and awkwardness. He was universally known as "Chas the Spaz."

The fact that his skin had mostly cleared up and his awkwardness was mostly a case of big-time shyness didn't matter. His reputation had been set since middle school. Chas was a guy you talked to when you were struggling with physics, not when you were looking for a good night out.

Karolina had joined chess club because she enjoyed playing against her father. She hoped that being a part of the club could help her figure out how to beat him.

At a lot of meetings she would play against Chas, and she noticed that when they were playing, he was a different kid. The chess game occupying one part of his mind freed up the rest to relax. When she talked to him she found him to be really smart (which everyone already knew) but also funny (which nobody would have guessed).

Sometimes they would sit and study together during lunch. But at no time did he ever indicate an interest beyond chess and studying. Then, one day he cornered her by her locker and asked her to prom. At first she thought he was going into some sort of asthmatic shock. He just stood there looking at her for what seemed like a minute before he was able to say, "Karolina Olsen, it would be my pleasure if you would allow me to escort you to the promenade."

It took her a moment to realize that "promenade" was the formal version of "prom." Then it took her a moment longer to figure out how to politely decline. But, before she could, she realized that Chas would be her ideal prom date. He was nice, well-mannered, and unlike most of the other guys at school, he wouldn't expect her to be some sort of Swedish sex goddess after the dance. Besides, he was a scientific genius—the ideal partner for her Jane Goodall approach to high school anthropology.

"Yes, Charles," she answered, using his full name to make it sound official. "Let's go to prom together."

She was surprised by the stretch limo. It didn't seem like a Chas kind of thing to do. When he got out, its size made him seem even smaller than usual.

She was also surprised by how cute he looked in his tuxedo. Although even from the house she could tell that his buttons and buttonholes were misaligned. He looked a little overwhelmed coming up the walkway and even took a break to bust out his inhaler. Karolina wondered if maybe she should have thought twice before saying yes.

When she opened the door, he just sort of stood there with

a pinch-me expression. She had on a strapless black baby-doll dress. He could hardly believe that he was her date. It was like giving a Ferrari to a kid with a learner's permit.

"Good evening, Chas," Karolina said with her cute Swedish accent.

It was the locker all over again. He just stood there for a moment, not really saying anything. Karolina thought she might have heard a little humming sound, but she wasn't sure.

"Chas?" she asked. "Is everything all right?"

"Of course," he said, snapping out it. "*Sa snygg du ar. Din klanning ar jatte vacker.*"

She gave him an odd look and cocked her head a little bit. "What did you say?"

"*Sa snygg du ar. Din klanning ar jatte vacker,*" he tried again. "I hope I'm not mispronouncing it. I've been practicing all day."

No," she replied with a beaming smile. "You said it perfectly."

He had just used flawless Swedish to say, "You look beautiful tonight. Your dress is stunning."

"Where did you learn that?"

"I called the Swedish embassy in Washington," he said sheepishly. "I explained to them that I was going to go to prom with a Swedish exchange student. And, I said I wanted to say at least one thing in Swedish. When they asked me what I wanted to say, I figured it was a lock that you'd look beautiful." He smiled. "Boy, was I right."

Karolina couldn't believe it. If anyone ever questioned why she was going to the prom with Chas Montgomery, she would tell them about this.

"Well," she responded. "*Du är en riktig snygging du med.*"

He had no idea what she was saying, and he didn't care. He was in heaven.

She translated, "You also look really good."

He didn't even try to pin the corsage on her. He just handed it to her.

The inside of the limo was fully tricked out. There was a mini fridge, a DVD/TV combo, and enough seating for at least eight. But with two they just seemed kind of lost in there. Chas was all the way over on one side, while she was on the other.

At least I don't have to worry about him copping a feel, she thought.

There was a long, awkward silence, and Karolina realized that she was going to have to do most of the work to keep the conversation flowing.

"You might want to fix your shirt," she said, pointing at his misaligned buttons.

He was totally clueless, so she reached over and tried to fix them for him.

All he saw was her unbuttoning his shirt. That set off more than a few alarms.

"You should know that I'm a virgin," he blurted out.

"What?"

"You should know that I'm a . . . virgin," he said ashamedly.

It took a moment, but she realized what he thought was happening. "I'm sorry. I wasn't trying to take your clothes off. I was just trying to fix your buttons."

When he looked down and saw the button, he blushed. "Nice," he said to himself. "Now she knows I'm a virgin."

This was not exactly a news bulletin, but she decided to boost his confidence a bit. "That *is* surprising," she said. "I guess you're just waiting for the right girl."

Any girl, he thought.

There was another silence before Karolina saw a DVD on the seat.

"What's that?" she asked.

"Oh," he said, handing it to her. "I remember you said that it was your favorite movie."

Karolina smiled as she looked at the cover of *Grease*. "Did you buy this for tonight?"

"No," he said. "It's my mom's favorite movie. She makes me watch it with her all the time."

"Your mother has good taste."

Chas decided to try a little small talk. Unfortunately, it came out sounding more like an English paper. "I couldn't help notice the similarities between you and the protagonist of the movie," he said.

She had no idea what he was talking about.

"In the film, Olivia Newton-John's character is Australian

and has to assimilate into American culture. Just as you're Swedish and doing likewise. That's not to say that Swedes and Australians are necessarily alike. Obviously there are great historical and contemporary differences. It's just that both you and she have to face many similar cultural hurdles."

Not exactly sweep-you-off-your-feet-romantic talk, but he was doing his best. "So," she said, deciding to go along with it. "If I'm Olivia Newton-John, I guess that makes you John Travolta."

He laughed so hard he made a snorting noise. "Yeah, right."

The limo pulled up to the country club where they were having dinner.

"Before we get out," he said to her. "I really want to thank you for going with me tonight. I mean, you could have gone with any guy. I just want you to know that I'll understand if when we're there, you want to hang out with other people. It won't hurt my feelings." (The last part was a lie.)

She looked at him for a moment. "We have a phrase in Swedish, *Den beskedlige får ingenting.* It means, 'The modest one gets nothing.' I think you think too little of yourself."

He didn't know what to say to her.

"Why did you ask me to go to the prom?"

"I've been asking myself that a lot lately," he answered. "I figured, if I was going to be rejected, I might as well get rejected by the prettiest girl in school."

"And what happened?" she asked with a smile.

He thought for a moment, unsure what she was driving at. Then he realized. "You said yes."

"That's right," Karolina responded. "I said yes. You're my date to my one and only prom. I'm counting on you to be my John Travolta."

Then, she leaned over and kissed him.

chapter **EIGHT**

Allison had absolutely no interest in being on the prom committee. The only reason she joined was to keep an eye on Molly. That's what best friends did. They got involved in each other's activities so they could spend time together and look out for each other.

Molly had done the same thing with soccer. A third-string goalie with virtually no chance of ever getting into a game, she sweated her way through two seasons of practices so she could cheer from the bench while Allison dominated on the field.

The two of them had been best friends since the seventh grade. It was a friendship born out of protest. It started when they both refused to dissect a frog in science class. They were sent to the office to be disciplined, and by the time they convinced the principal to ban all dissections at school, they knew they made a great team.

Allison's laid-back attitude was the perfect fit for Molly's uptight tendencies. Just as she did during the walk-through at the American Legion hall, Allison was always there to knock some sense into Molly when she started having a meltdown. Likewise, Molly was able to inject some organization into Allison's otherwise casual approach to life. It was Molly who made sure Allison remembered to study for exams and completed all of her big assignments in time.

Despite all of Molly's best efforts, many aspects of Allison's life defied organizing. For Christmas she gave Allison the same *Too Hot to Handle* fireman calendar that she had gotten on her birthday. But, while Molly had been excited about getting a new calendar, Allison was only excited by the firefighters. She rendered the calendar part useless when she detached all the pictures and hung them side by side on her wall.

"You're missing the point," Molly pointed out at the time. "It's a calendar. You can organize your life."

"No, Molly, you're missing the point," Allison corrected. "If I use it as a calendar, then eleven of those brave young men are facing the wrong way."

In addition to being disorganized, Allison was also a total slob. The room that the firemen of the *Too Hot to Handle* calendar looked out over was as bad as the after-picture of a three-alarm blaze. Clothes and paper were strewn in every direction, which was why Allison was frantically searching for one of her shoes.

"Are you ready yet?" her mother called from downstairs.

Allison cringed. Her mother was always on her case about the mess. "I'm just finishing my hair," she lied.

"If you're doing your hair, why do I hear you digging around in your closet?"

Damn, her mother had good ears. "It's not me," Allison tried. "It's the dog."

"Nice try." Her mother laughed. "But the dog's down here with me."

Allison thought for a moment. "I've got nothing."

"Just hurry up. They'll be here any moment, and you still need to set the table."

To save money, and to give the evening a little something extra, Allison's mother was preparing a fancy sit-down dinner for a few of the couples. Allison's grandparents ran an Italian restaurant in New York, and her mother had learned to be a great cook. For special occasions like this, she made the most amazing baked chicken stuffed with rice, vegetables, and mozzarella cheese. On the menu at the restaurant it was called *Pollo Pirlo*.

The smell was amazing, even upstairs, where Allison stood in a closet surrounded by old soccer cleats and tennis shoes. Finally she found the missing shoe and rushed downstairs to the dining room.

She quickly started putting out her parents' wedding china. For the dinner Allison had invited her two best friends and their dates. That meant she had to put out six place settings, which suddenly presented a problem.

"How should I do this?" she called into the kitchen. "If I put the couples together, then one side has four and the other side has two."

Allison looked down and moved a place setting across the table. "But if I put three on a side, one couple isn't sitting together."

Mrs. Pirlo came in from the kitchen to help. "Maybe you can put the boys on one side and the girls . . ." She stopped midsentence when she saw Allison.

"What's the matter?" Allison asked, suddenly panicked. "Did I get something on my dress?"

"No, nothing's wrong," Mrs. Pirlo said, about to tear up at the mere sight of her daughter in her prom dress. (In addition to the cooking skills, she also possessed the entire spectrum of Italian emotions.)

"Mom, you promised you wouldn't."

"I can't help it," she said, choking back the tears. "Look at you."

Allison was wearing a gold halter dress that they found during a trip to New York to visit her grandparents. It was dressy but still comfortable.

Now Allison was about to cry. "You're going to make me ruin my makeup."

Just then there was a knock at the door. This only made things worse.

"Mom," Allison implored. "Real people are here."

"Just one hug?"

"Okay," she said with a shrug. "But just one." Her mother engulfed her in her arms, and they both let out a little sob.

There was another knock, and Allison had to pry herself free. As she walked to the door, she saw Peter's car through the window and her heart started racing.

She'd had a crush on Peter ever since they sat next to each other in sophomore English. Some girls thought he was a little geeky (okay, he *was* a little geeky), but for Allison that was just part of the charm. There was never any doubt that he was the one guy she wanted to go with to her senior prom.

Before answering the door, she checked herself in the mirror to make sure her mom's hug hadn't caused any crinkling and that there weren't any leftover tears.

She took a deep breath and opened the door to see Peter smiling broadly. He looked great in his tuxedo, just as he did every time she had imagined this moment. It nearly took her breath away.

Unfortunately, Peter's date looked great too.

Despite her endless crush on him, Allison had never built up the courage to actually tell Peter how she felt. He had no idea. Instead, she became his close friend and confidante—the girl he came to for advice when he was having trouble with girls.

"You look great," Peter said.

"Thanks," Allison replied, trying not to die right then and there. "You both look wonderful. Come on in."

Peter's date was Kiki Mott. She was tall, pretty, and dumb as a post. (When *The Catcher in the Rye* was assigned in English class, she complained that she wasn't interested in reading about baseball.) She was also a little on the slutty side. Allison figured that this was the main reason Peter had asked her.

"Let me see Pete," Allison's mom said as she barged into the room. "Awww, look how gorgeous you are."

"Mom!" Allison implored.

Peter didn't mind in the least. After three years, he was more than used to Allison's mom. "Not as gorgeous as you, Mrs. Pirlo."

"Who's the hot date?"

Allison was tempted to say, "One of the leading whores of the junior class."

"This is Kiki," Pete said, handling the introductions. "Kiki, this is the one and only Mrs. Pirlo."

"Nice to meet you," Kiki said, unsure what to make of Allison's mom.

"Nice to meet you, Kiki."

Before they could get settled, there was another knock on the door. It was Allison's date Warren. Allison liked him, but there was absolutely no chemistry between them. They both played saxophone in the marching band but that was about all they had in common. She had agreed to go with him strictly as friends—a point she reiterated on several occasions.

She probably wouldn't have even said yes if she hadn't

been so worried. With no boyfriend or boyfriend prospect—and with no chance of admitting her true feelings to Peter—Allison was looking at the very real chance of not having a date for prom.

Apparently, he didn't fully understand what going "as friends" meant. When he saw Allison, he told her, "You look hot," and gave her a big kiss that caught everyone off guard.

There was an awkward silence, and Allison was completely embarrassed.

"Everyone, come on into the family room," Mom said, coming to the rescue. "Dinner will be ready in a few minutes."

When they got into the family room, Warren sat down on the love seat, which Allison bypassed in favor of her father's recliner.

"So, how long have you two been going out?" Kiki asked.

"We're just friends," Allison said.

"For now," Warren said with a wink at Peter.

Allison was in hell.

The last couple to arrive was Molly and Ben, whom Allison was dying to meet. When Molly thought about backing out of the whole blind-date thing, Allison had convinced her by saying, "You never know. He might be the one."

"You must be Allison," he said. "I'm Ben. It's very nice to meet you."

Allison looked up at his dreamy eyes and was beyond envious. "Nice to meet you, Ben. Please come in."

"Trade you," Allison whispered to Molly as she passed by. Molly just shook her head.

Molly handled all of the introductions in the living room. Ben scored major points when he gave Mrs. Pirlo some flowers he'd picked up at the florist.

"How thoughtful," she said, touched. "I'll put these on the table."

"Those are from all of us," Peter joked, wishing he'd thought to bring some.

"Yeah," Ben played along. "Everybody chipped in. I'm just the one who picked them up."

Mrs. Pirlo put them in a vase at the center of the table. Everything looked perfect. Allison was happy she'd opted to put three settings on each side. She sat across from Warren (where at least he couldn't touch her) and next to Peter (where she could imagine he was her date).

As they sat down, Allison turned to Molly. Earlier they had worked out a code so that they could secretly rate Ben on a scale from one to ten.

"How many different pairs of shoes did you try on when you were getting ready?" Allison asked.

Molly thought for a moment. "Six or seven," she said, cutting the rating a little lower than she actually felt.

Allison wasn't buying it. "I bet you tried on at least eight, maybe nine," she said pointedly.

"How about you?" Molly asked, indicating Warren.

"Just one," she said.

Molly smiled and tried her best to keep from laughing.

chapter NINE

6:11 P.M.
1 hour and 49 minutes until prom

Jenna didn't have any delusions about being named prom queen. Like everybody else, she was certain Victoria had that title all wrapped up. Still, there were some advantages just to being named to the court. For her, the best part had to do with Crescent Lake Country Club. Jenna lived only a mile from the big black gates that marked the entrance to the club, but it might as well have been a hundred miles. She'd never been inside.

But now, because she was on the prom court, she was riding in the backseat of a limousine and a guard was waving her through those gates. She was about to have dinner in the most exclusive spot in town and that felt just right.

Everything about Crescent Lake Country Club was exclusive—especially the dining room. To eat the Smoked Salmon Napoleon, Venison Carpaccio, or Panfried Guinea Fowl with a Summer Berry

Sauce, you had to be either a member or the guest of a member.

An exception was made on prom night. (Not for regular students—that would invite anarchy—but an exception for the elite students on the prom court.) It had been tradition for the members of the court to eat together at the club for as long as anyone could remember. To abide by the rules, the students were officially listed as guests of the club president, who came by at the start of dinner to pose for a group picture and who stopped by at the end to pick up the tab.

It had also been tradition for the members of the court to pretend to like one another. It was this tradition that Victoria was having trouble pulling off. Unlike her best friend, Jenna, who was in heaven, Victoria was in a little corner of hell.

The night that was supposed to mark her greatest achievement was turning out to be a major pain. The girls nominated for queen were placed at one table with their dates, while the boys nominated for king were put at another with theirs. (This meant that Victoria and Jenna were seated at a table with Victoria's archenemy, Karolina, the Swedish sex symbol; her joke of a date, Chas the Spaz; and Rachel, who, by Victoria's account, had no business being anywhere near the prom court.) Worst of all, her boyfriend, Matt, wasn't back from his stupid baseball game yet.

Over at the kings table, they were already eating their appetizers—or at least attempting to eat them. One guy was trying to act refined and eat escargot, but he looked like he was about to bolt for the bathroom. Another was trying to figure out which utensil to use to eat caviar. Still, they were laughing about it and having a good time.

At the queen's table, they were not laughing, and they were not eating. Victoria insisted they wait for Matt to arrive before ordering. (She also insisted the president wait for Matt to arrive before they posed for the picture. She got away with it because she was the only one of the group who was also a club member.)

"He'll be here any moment," she assured the waiter. "He just sent me a text."

The waiter was impeccably dressed in a dinner jacket and bow tie. Even though he knew it was a total lie, he nodded politely and smiled. "Of course," he said. "I'll get you all some more bread for the time being."

"Could you get me some more bottled water?" Rachel asked with a smile. (She was not about to let Victoria's mood affect her night. She was living it up.)

He smiled at her. "It would be my pleasure."

As he walked away, Rachel turned to the others. "As nice and as well dressed as he is, maybe I should ask if he wants to go with me tonight."

For the first time there were some laughs at the table.

"Of course, if Matt doesn't show up," Rachel continued, "I can always go with you, Victoria."

This brought bigger laughs, although Victoria did not find

it the least bit funny. She just gave Rachel an angry look. "I wouldn't go to prom with a girl," she snapped.

"I was just joking," Rachel answered.

"I don't find deviant lifestyles to be humorous," Victoria said, bringing the conversation to a halt. There was a prolonged silence before she got up to go to the restroom. "I'll be right back," she announced. She waited for a moment until Jenna got the clue and got up to follow.

"Me too," she said.

Once they were out of earshot, everyone at the table let out a huge sigh of relief.

"What is that girl's problem?" Karolina said, shaking her head.

She wasn't really looking for an answer, but Chas offered one. "Do you really want to know? Because I have an idea."

This caught everyone's attention.

"Really?" Kirby asked. He didn't know Chas very well, but he knew he was smart.

"She's jealous," he answered.

This brought laughs.

"I'm serious," he said. "I think she's jealous of all of you."

"You think Victoria is jealous of me?" Rachel asked, dumbfounded. "Of all of us?"

"She's jealous of Jenna, because Jenna is just as popular, but she's not a bitch," he explained. "People really like her."

Kirby smiled proudly.

"She's jealous of Karolina," he continued, "because Karolina is prettier and smarter."

"You're just saying that because you're my date," Karolina said.

"No," Kirby agreed. "You're much better looking."

Then Chas looked at Rachel. "And you she's most jealous of," he offered. "Because you don't care what people think and that's all she cares about."

There was a moment of profound silence, as though Chas might really be on to something. Then Rachel added, "Personally, I think her underwear's too tight."

This brought huge laughs.

Jenna couldn't believe how many wood paneled rooms there were. She couldn't figure out which one was the bathroom.

"Here," Victoria said as she opened the door to a room with a sign reading "Ladies' Lounge."

Jenna was amazed by how nice it was inside. There was a large sitting room with antique furniture and floor-to-ceiling mirrors.

"Wow, this is sweet," she said with a hint of jealousy in her voice. It hurt that she had never been to the club before. Victoria and her family had been members for years but had never invited her to be a guest.

"I just had to get out of there," Victoria said as she sat down on one of the couches. "So far this night is just total hell, don't you think?"

Even though Jenna was having a good time, she knew better

than to say it. She just played along with Victoria. "Nightmare."

"Did you hear Rachel hitting on me?" she asked.

Jenna gave her an uncertain look. "What are you talking about?"

"That comment she made about going together," she said. "I've always told you she was a lesbian."

"I'm pretty certain it was just a joke."

"No," Victoria said. "A joke is bringing Chas the Spaz to prom. What's the deal with that?"

"I don't know. He's being kind of cute," Jenna said. "He even looks pretty good in his tuxedo. And he's so attentive. Did you see how he pulled out her chair for her? Or how he stood up when she went to the ladies' room?"

"Of course he's being attentive," Victoria said. "He's just grateful to be here. It's probably the first date he's ever been on."

Victoria stood up and looked at herself in the mirror for a moment.

"Do you honestly think that Rachel is gay?" Jenna asked.

"I told you about that New Year's party," Victoria said.

"You were kind of sketchy about it."

"I saw her try to make a move on a girl," Victoria said, making a disgusted face. "It was grotesque."

"I was at that same party," Jenna offered. "I didn't see a thing."

Victoria stopped and looked at her. "Consider yourself lucky."

Victoria went back to checking her dress in the mirror. It was ivory with an empire waist, a black lace bust, and a low back. "I love this dress."

"It's great," Jenna said. "You look really hot."

"I do, don't I?" Victoria replied rather than return the compliment. "Let's go see if my idiot boyfriend has finally arrived."

When they walked back into the dining room, they could see Matt sitting at the table.

"Thank God, he's finally here."

He was turned away from them, but they could see that he was animatedly telling a story to everyone at the table. Whatever it was, they were eating it up.

"So he hits this weak-ass grounder right back toward the pitcher," Matt said, telling them about the game. "And he throws the ball to me, right? So I've got to block the plate . . ."

Just then Victoria and Jenna reached the table.

"You gotta hear this," Rachel said excitedly. "Matt's telling us how he won the game."

Matt turned to face Victoria, and for the first time she saw his black eye. If they weren't in the middle of the club, she would have screamed. Instead she paused for a moment to maintain her composure.

"What happened to you?" she demanded.

"It was great," Rachel said. "There was a collision at home plate . . ."

Victoria cut her right off. "I wasn't talking to you."

"It looks worse than it is," Matt assured her.

"Good, because it looks terrible."

"Don't worry," he continued. "I'll be fine. It will heal right up in a couple of days."

"Too bad the prom pictures aren't being taken in a couple of days."

The others were dumbfounded.

"You can't be serious," Rachel pleaded. "He saved the . . ."

Before she could finish, Matt gave her a look and shook his head.

Luckily, the waiter came to the rescue to take everyone's order.

"Please, tell me. What can I get you?"

Rachel was tempted to say "Another table."

chapter **TEN**

Peter drove his teachers crazy. It wasn't that he was diffi-cult in the classroom. (He was always polite, funny, and charming, and his teachers all loved him.) The prob-lem was that he never worked particularly hard. He believed in doing just enough to get by.

Every now and then, he'd fall below even that low standard, and his teachers would have to do something drastic to get his attention. Recently, his English teacher returned a book report with no corrections—just a grade of F and a note saying, "Do your parents know you're not going to graduate?"

That was enough to spur him into a flurry of studying that saw him ace two straight tests and pull up his grade to a low C just in time for report cards. That's the part that drove them crazy. They knew he could be a top student if he just applied himself.

Peter followed the path of least resistance in his personal life, too. And, so far, it worked perfectly. The prom was a prime example. Allison had invited him to join her group, which meant he didn't have to worry about renting a limo or even paying for dinner. (Which, by the way, was delicious.) His date was smoking hot and so far had given him every indication that she was more than willing to give him a memorable night.

All he had to do was rent a tux and show up. Everything else was going to take care of itself. He just didn't understand why some people made life so complicated.

Allison, meanwhile, was trying to balance a couple of conflicting emotions. First of all, it was killing her to see Peter going to prom with someone else. But she knew she had no one to blame but herself. She hadn't told him how she felt, and as a result, she was stuck with Warren, who still didn't seem to get the idea of what going "as friends" meant.

She had to rebuff his attempt to play footsie at the same time she was regaling everyone with the story of Molly's breakdown during the morning walk-through at the American Legion hall. She stressed the part about the girl who had a twitching fit and knew Tae Kwon Do.

Everyone at the table was laughing, including Molly.

"And I could tell it was going to happen the second I saw her face," Allison continued. "I know all of Molly's expressions."

"Really," Molly said, joking but also not wanting to be any more embarrassed in front of Ben. "Do you know this one?" She flashed Allison an "enough is enough" look.

"Yes, I know that one well," Allison said, suddenly ending the story. "So, who's ready for dessert?"

The boys instantly shot their hands into the air.

"Molly, why don't you help me?" Allison asked as she stood up. The two of them went into the kitchen and started gossiping the moment the door shut.

"Oh my God," Allison whispered. "Ben is serious arm candy."

"Cut it out," she said. Then, after a moment, she added, "He is cute, isn't he?"

Allison nodded big-time as she pulled a container of spumoni out of the freezer. They scooped it into small bowls while they continued talking.

"He's nice, too," Allison added.

"He really is," Molly said. "Now, is it my imagination, or did I catch you playing footsie with Warren during dinner?"

"Don't even start," Allison said. "I do not know what is up with that boy. I told him we were going only as friends, and so far he has planted a kiss on me, twice rubbed up against me, and then the foot thing. I'm going to kill him. I swear to God."

Just then Warren came into the room.

"Ooh, sweets getting sweets," he said, laying on his pathetic brand of charm as he tried to cozy up to Allison.

She blocked the move by handing him a couple of bowls.

"Can you carry these out?"

He reluctantly took them. "Sure," he said as he headed back toward the dining room. "Don't worry, I'll be back."

Once he got out of the room, Allison turned back to Molly. "I don't know what I'm going to do."

"I think he's drunk."

Allison thought for a moment. "That makes total sense," she said. "I hadn't even considered that." Allison never drank, and as a result was not good at spotting it in others.

"Any chance that Kiki's drunk?" Molly asked.

"Just stupid," Allison said, shaking her head. "Of course, I don't think Peter's looking for stimulating conversation."

"No," joked Molly. "He's just looking for someone to stimulate his peter."

"You're killing me," Allison said. "You're my best friend and you're killing me."

After dessert, the six of them headed out back to the patio to pose for pictures. On the way outside, Ben pulled Molly aside.

"Are you having a good time?" he asked.

"Absolutely," she said.

"So tell me, what's the deal with Allison and Peter?"

Molly smiled. "That's a very good question."

"Was there something between them before?"

"She wishes. Allison's been in love with Peter forever," she explained. "Except, she's never said anything because she's worried it will scare him away."

"That's too bad," he said. "I think she'd be better for him than Miss Brain Freeze."

PRAMA

87

Just then Allison popped back inside. "Come on," she said. "Let's get these done before Mom starts crying again."

On the patio, Allison's mom had set up a couple of places where they could pose for pictures. First they all posed together. Then there was a glamorous shot of the girls, followed by a humorous one of the boys. (They flexed their muscles like they were body builders.)

For each couple, Mrs. Pirlo had picked out a spot overlooking some trees in her backyard. Molly and Ben went first. When he put his arm around her, Molly couldn't help but notice how perfectly she fit next to him. He was the ideal height—definitely a good sign.

The next to go were Warren and Allison. When he leaned in to put his arm around her, she definitely smelled alcohol on his breath. When his hand wandered south of her waist and onto her butt, she "accidentally" drove her heel down onto his foot.

The last couple to pose was Peter and Kiki. She slutted right up next to him, pressing her chest against his. It was almost more than Allison could bear. As if it wasn't bad enough that she was stuck with a loser date, now she had to watch her dream guy posing with a tramp on her patio.

Ben could tell she was hurting.

"Oh my God," he said, flying by the seat of his pants. "I almost forgot about the psych experiment."

"What?" Molly asked.

"In my psychology class we're supposed to do a body-language experiment with these pictures," he said, hoping it sounded believable.

"What kind of experiment?" Peter asked.

"Body language. I'm supposed to get a picture of each couple and another picture of each of us posing with someone else. Then, everyone in the class is supposed to guess who is really with whom. Since they don't know you, the only way they can tell is by body language."

"I think you lost me," Molly said.

"It's easy," he answered. "We just need to each pose with someone we're not going with. I'll take a picture with Kiki, you can take one with Warren, and *Allison can take one with Peter.*"

He said the last part with emphasis, and suddenly Molly realized what he was trying to do.

"I love this idea," she said, trying to sound convincing. "Come on, Warren, take a picture with me."

Before Warren even got a chance to say anything, Molly had her arm around him and Mrs. Pirlo was taking their picture.

Next, Ben brought Kiki over. "We really have to sell it or the experiment won't work," he told her as he put his arm around her. "The picture has to look legit."

Kiki was clueless as to what was going on, but that was a normal condition for her, so she happily snuggled in next to Ben and they took a picture.

That left one more picture to take.

Allison sheepishly looked over at Peter. "I guess that leaves us."

They were tentative at first, but Peter put a solid arm around her.

"Remember to sell it," Ben reminded them. "Make it look real."

Peter pulled her closer, and for a moment, Allison was in heaven. She knew that when she got to college, this would be the picture she'd put on her bookshelf. Screw reality. This would be the memory she would want to keep forever.

Her mom took the picture and a surprising thing happened. Peter's hold lasted a little bit longer than it needed to.

As they headed back into the house, Molly leaned over to Ben and whispered, "I didn't know what you were doing at first, but that was pretty cool."

Ben smiled. "I know—I really wanted to have my picture taken with Kiki. She's hot."

Molly laughed and slugged Ben in the arm. Then she noticed Allison looking at the camera. She had scanned through the images in the display until she'd come to the one of her and Peter.

When she was done, she looked over at Molly and smiled.

"Ten pairs," Allison said, reverting to their earlier rating code. "I think you tried on at least ten different pairs of shoes."

chapter ELEVEN

7:27 P.M.
33 minutes until prom

Chas was going to major in computer science because computers made sense to him. They could be relied on. People, on the other hand, were completely unreasonable.

He'd given up solving the mystery of why the most attractive girl in the school had agreed to go to prom with him. (To understand Karolina, he'd need to model some chaos theory equations.) Now he was trying to figure out Victoria.

They were just finishing a delicious meal at an exclusive country club. She was smart, attractive, and about to win yet another award. Her boyfriend was one of the most popular guys at school.

Yet, somehow, she was miserable.

She had sulked through the entire meal all because Matt had

a black eye that was going to mess up her picture. (If Chas ever got a black eye doing something cool like Matt did, he'd get as much photographic proof as possible.)

At least some people were making sense. Rachel was having the time of her life. So far she had eaten the shrimp cocktail, the wedge salad, and most of her Chicken Provençal and loved every bite of it.

"It's good, isn't it?" Chas said to Rachel.

She beamed. "Delicious."

"Mine's great," Karolina added.

Kirby looked over at Chas. "What are you going to study in college?"

"Computers," he answered.

Kirby smiled. He wondered what the future held for a guy like Chas. He'd been picked on forever, but Kirby knew Chas would have the last laugh when he got out of town and made some serious money.

"Where are you going to go?" Rachel asked him.

"Stanford or Duke," he said. "Probably Stanford."

"Wow. That's great."

"I was thinking about going to Stanford," Matt said, happy to jump into the conversation. "Only it turns out you have to be smart."

Everybody laughed. (Everybody but Victoria.) "What about you, Rachel?" Matt continued. "Where are you off to next year?"

"I'm going to major in English at Dartmouth," she said, still loving the sound of it.

"That's great," he said. "It doesn't surprise me at all. Your columns for the paper are the best."

"Thanks," she said, genuinely touched.

Matt turned to the others. "You wouldn't believe what she went through to do the one on the football team—'My Life as a Bench Warmer,' right?"

"That was awesome," Kirby added.

Rachel couldn't believe they remembered.

"She came to practice and did the whole thing. Wore the pads, ran the laps. She even did a blocking drill."

This was entirely too much attention being paid to someone other than Victoria.

"You better watch out," she interrupted acidly. "I hear those Ivy League schools are full of lesbians looking to take advantage of cute little things like you."

This caught everyone off guard and brought the good mood to a screeching halt.

"Really?" Matt said, trying to come to the rescue. "I heard they were full of really smart people. Congratulations, Rach, really."

Obviously hurt, Rachel forced a smile. "Thanks."

"*Din satkäring!*" Karolina said, calling Victoria a bitch under her breath.

Just then the club president came back to take the long-delayed picture. First he took a picture with the girls, which left

Chas alone with Matt and Kirby. Matt was obviously relieved to have Victoria momentarily away.

Normally Chas might be intimidated. But Matt and Kirby had never been anything but nice to him. They weren't friends, but they weren't bullies.

"That's pretty cool that you're going to go study computers," Kirby said to him.

"Absolutely," Matt answered. "And it's more than cool that you're taking Karolina to the prom. Hats off, dude."

Chas let out another snorting laugh. "I know. It just doesn't make any sense, does it?"

Matt gave him a skeptical look. "It makes all the sense in the world."

He gave him a pat on the back, and they all headed over to pose for the group picture, and for the first time in his life, Chas felt like one of the guys.

The picture started to turn ugly when the photographer tried to pose Victoria next to Rachel. Victoria wouldn't have anything to do with that, and Jenna quickly jumped in between them so that things wouldn't get worse.

After the picture incident, Rachel, who had been having so much fun, suddenly got very quiet. She didn't say a word during dessert. And she didn't hang around with the others while they waited for their cars to come up.

She just hurried off to her car.

Matt and Kirby felt bad for her. But it was Chas who rushed

to the rescue. The night had already given him some newfound confidence. He charged right out and caught up with her as she was getting into her car.

"Rachel," he said, reaching for the door so that she couldn't shut it.

"I can't talk right now," she said. When she looked up at him, her eyes were filled with tears.

"Where are you going?" he asked.

"I'm going home," she answered. "Where I belong."

"No. You can't do that. You can't let yourself get bullied. If anyone knows that, it's me."

"Look at you," she said. "You're with the hottest girl in school."

"I know. And I need your help."

"What are you talking about?"

"I feel like an idiot riding around in that huge limousine alone with Karolina. She's too much woman for me."

Despite her tears, Rachel let out a brief laugh.

"Come with us. We'll have a great time. I promise."

"I appreciate it," she offered. "But I'm really not in the mood."

"Forget your mood," he implored her. "That is way too nice a dress to waste. Besides, you need to go for your column."

Rachel thought for a moment. Other than dealing with Victoria, she was having a great time.

"Okay," she answered, wiping away the tears.

Moments later, Chas, Rachel, and Karolina were all piled into the back of the limousine. Rachel was still a bit upset, so the others were quiet for a moment.

As they started to pull out, they saw Matt and Victoria through the window. Now that they were away from everyone, Victoria was letting him have it over the black eye.

"I don't believe it," Chas said.

"What?"

"I don't believe that I feel pity for Matt Hall."

chapter TWELVE

I t looks freaking awesome!"

That was Allison's unvarnished opinion as Ben pulled the lame-o into the parking lot at the American Legion hall. In keeping with the "Hollywood Dreams" theme, the outside of the building had been made to look like the world premiere of a movie. Two big searchlights pointed into the sky, and a red carpet stretched from the front door to a point where limos were dropping off students in tuxedoes and gowns. To complete the effect, four sophomores from the drama club pretended to be paparazzi and took pictures of the people as they walked the red carpet.

Peter tried to scrunch forward from the backseat so he could look out the windshield. "It really does look good," he said.

"Wait until you see the inside," Allison assured them. "It only gets better."

The parking lot was a total zoo. There were limos and sports cars. One couple even arrived by horse-drawn carriage. Ben was having trouble finding a spot.

"Around the back," Molly told him. "I thought ahead."

Ben pulled the car behind the building, where there was an orange cone reserving a space. A sign on the cone said "Prom Committee Only."

"Nice thinking," Ben said as she got out to move the cone.

"Yeah," Allison added. "Sometimes that anal-retentive stuff pays off."

Ben pulled the lame-o into the spot, and everybody started getting out.

"Sorry about it being so cramped," he said as Peter climbed out of the backseat.

"Not a problem," Peter said. "Thanks for driving."

As they headed toward the front of the building and the red carpet, one person was lagging.

"You okay?" Ben asked Warren, who was leaning against the car with his head down. "I'm fine," he said. "Go on without me. I'll catch up."

"We can't," Allison said. "It's one ticket per couple. We've got to go in together."

"Okay," he responded. "Just give me a sec then."

So far, prom was not going as Warren had planned. It had gotten off track earlier in the day. He had a tendency to get impatient before big events. When he was eleven and played in the Little League championship, he was so excited to wear his uniform that he'd put it on first thing in the morning, even though the game was late that afternoon. He spent the entire day in his room, pretending to be Alex Rodriguez. (He struck out three times and the team lost 12–1.)

When he first got promoted into the marching band, he did the same thing with his ridiculous purple-and-gold band uniform. He put it on hours before the game and marched around his room imagining that he was the great jazz saxophonist John Coltrane. (As if Trane ever played the sax in a giant fuzzy hat.)

Today it was the tuxedo.

He just couldn't wait to put it on. He was dressed and ready to go hours before he needed to be. This time, instead of A-Rod or Coltrane, he imagined he was James Bond.

"Sadler. Warren Sadler," he practiced in the mirror about a dozen times. When he got bored with that, he decided to do something that he had resisted with both the Little League and band uniforms. He decided to leave the protective cocoon of his bedroom.

He went down to the convenience store where his older brother Kevin was working part-time to pay his way through community college.

Kevin fancied himself a ladies' man, and Warren wanted some advice about the evening. He was especially concerned with how he should deal with Allison's insistence that they were going "only as friends."

"Total bullshit," his brother assured him. "She's just saying that for insurance. If you come in there and flash the Sadler charm, she'll want to be more than friends. Trust me."

This sounded good to Warren—except he wasn't particularly skilled with the Sadler charm. So his brother gave him a quick lesson using whatever was on hand at the 'Round the Clock, Stop and Shop.

Warren practiced all of his romantic moves on a cardboard cut-out of a girl in a bikini selling light beer. He practiced his dance moves on an ancient Dance Dance Revolution game in the back. (Kevin rigged it so he didn't have to use any quarters.) Then, in the bathroom, he discovered a vending machine called the ScentSplash that had three little jets that dispense knockoff versions of upscale colognes. Unable to decide if he should go for the fake Aramis, Polo, or Drakkar, he opted to make a mix of all three.

Before he left, his brother treated him to a couple of beers. "To take the edge off." He wasn't drunk, but he was definitely light-headed and bold.

Despite his brother's intensive training, none of his plans were working out. The moves that literally swept the cardboard girl off her feet were all getting shot down by Allison.

She still seemed very committed to her "just friends" concept.

More importantly, the beer and the mixture of colognes were beginning to take a heavy toll on him. Add carsickness from being crammed into the back of Ben's Lincoln Continental, and Warren was not doing well.

After a few moments of fresh air, he was able to build the strength to put on a happy face. He smiled and joined the others as they walked down the red carpet.

Allison was safe. He wasn't going to be putting any moves on her for the time being. He needed to save all of his concentration to make it down the red carpet without falling on his face. Hopefully, once he got inside, he'd be able to find a nice dark corner where he could get it together.

"Smile!" shouted one of the paparazzi as she jumped in front of him and snapped a picture. The startling effect almost did Warren in.

Luckily, he was far enough behind the others that they didn't realize he was struggling. They were having too much fun.

"This is going to be a blast," Kiki said as she gripped Peter's arm.

Ben smiled at Molly. "I know we just got here, but this is the best prom I've ever been to."

"This is the only prom you've ever been to," she reminded him.

"True, but you still should be really proud," he said. "You're, like, the mayor of prom."

She smiled. "Mayor's not quite the same as queen," she added with a shrug.

"Yeah," Ben responded. "But the mayor never gets the guillotine when the people revolt."

"Good point."

The line started to back up as they neared the door. Tickets were being taken and members of the faculty were welcoming students.

"Who are they?" Ben asked, pointing to them.

"Mostly administrators," Molly answered. "A couple of deans over there. That's Principal Ragans."

She pointed at a man who was leaning in to hug a girl in a big fluffy dress.

"He seems friendly," Ben said. Then he looked for a moment longer. "Really friendly."

Now the principal was throwing his arm around one of the boys and giving him a hearty handshake and laugh.

"Yeah," Peter added. "What's up with that?"

Molly and Allison shared a knowing look, which Ben caught.

"Wait a second. You two know something."

Molly nodded. "They're not just welcoming students," she informed them. "They're on alcohol patrol. They use the welcoming as a cover to lean in close so they can smell everyone's breath."

Ben laughed. "I guess that's easier than a Breathalyzer."

"What do you mean, *alcohol patrol*?" Warren asked, suddenly interested in the conversation.

"Read the ticket," Allison said, holding theirs up for him to see.

Warren tried to focus on it but was having trouble.

"I forgot my glasses. Could you read it for me?"

Allison rolled her eyes and started reading. "Prom is a one hundred percent drug- and alcohol-free event. Any student who violates this policy will be removed from the prom and will face appropriate discipline."

Now Warren was reeling. His night had gone from bad to worse. Getting kicked out of prom would be bad enough. But appropriate discipline sounded really bad.

"Have you been drinking, Warren?" Allison asked him point-blank. "Because if they smell it, they'll bust you."

Warren was at a crossroads. If he bolted now, the night would be a total waste. If he just sucked it up and got inside, he could sit down for a few minutes and do just fine.

"No, no," he said. "I wouldn't drink before a school event. What am I? A moron? I just feel a little sick to my stomach. It must have been something I ate."

This almost set Allison off completely, considering they'd just eaten a meal her mother had spent all day preparing. Molly reached over and held her back.

"You shouldn't have waited in line," the principal said to Molly when she reached the front. "After all, this is your party." He didn't even bother to lean in on her. He knew she was clean.

"Dr. Ragans, this is my date, Ben Bauer. He's a student over at West High."

"Good choice," the principal told him. "The girls at Fletcher are much smarter than the ones at West." As he made the joke, he leaned in to smell Ben's breath.

"Sorry about the garlic," Ben whispered.

The principal smiled and moved on to Peter and Kiki.

Warren got more and more nervous as each person in the group was greeted. He'd gone four years without ever speaking to the principal. Finally everyone had gone but him.

Warren closed his eyes and said a silent prayer.

"I recognize the face but can't place the name," the principal said to Warren. "Saxophone, right?"

That's when Warren threw up on the principal.

chapter THIRTEEN

8:06 P.M.

The Fletcher High School Junior-Senior Prom officially began at eight o'clock, when the deejay played Pink's "Get the Party Started." Ben guessed that it was one of the two most common prom kickoff songs, along with "Let's Get it Started" by the Black Eyed Peas. (Personally, he would have used "Start Me Up" by the Rolling Stones, but that was just him.)

But while the first song may have been predictable, nothing else about the start of prom was. Warren Sadler was already passed out on a couch in an office while an assistant principal called his parents to inform them that they needed to come down to the American Legion hall and pick him up.

There aren't records on such things, but it was the earliest ejection in the history of the Fletcher prom. Pink was less than twenty seconds into the song when the "moment of vomit" occurred. Ironically, she had just sung the words "I'm coming up" when Mrs. Pirlo's stuffed chicken started coming up all over Dr. Ragans.

"The eruption," as it would come to be known, sent Molly's group into three different directions. Peter was instructed by Dr. Ragans to keep an eye on Warren until his parents arrived. (His main job was to hold a wastebasket nearby in case there was a relapse.) Peter didn't think this was fair, but the principal was in no mood to hear about fair and unfair at the moment.

Horrified at what her date had just done, Allison rushed for cover in the girls' room. Amazingly, it was already packed with girls checking out their hair and dishing on who looked bad. By the time Molly and Kiki caught up with her, Allison was already holed up in the handicapped stall. Luckily, there was room for all three in there. (Kiki may not have been a close friend, but the Girl Code called for instant action in the case of emergencies.)

That left Ben all alone, guarding three purses and a table for eight. Like she did with the parking spot, Molly had picked out the table the night before. It was close to the food and the dance floor, provided a good view of the entrance, and was directly beneath an air-conditioning vent. In other words, it was the one table that everyone wanted.

During the decorate-a-thon, she had placed a sign on it that said RESERVED. Unfortunately, it didn't look particularly official. And it didn't carry much weight in a situation where Ben didn't know anybody and there weren't nearly as many tables as there were people. (Molly would later explain that the idea behind the scarcity of tables was to get more people onto the dance floor.)

"Sorry, table's taken," he said whenever someone tried to sit down. Sometimes he'd point to the RESERVED sign and just kind of shrug. Whatever he did, the response was pretty much the same. The person would shoot him a dirty look and grumble under his or her breath. Ben did his best to smile and act friendly.

It helped a little when he arranged the purses to block off a "saved zone." But, eventually, he resorted to telling people, "Watch out, Warren Sadler just threw up over there and I'm not sure they cleaned it all up."

That did the trick better than any purse or sign could ever do.

One shortcoming of the American Legion hall was that its girls' room was much too small for the number of girls who would need it during the night. Allison had scored a major coup when she nabbed the handicapped stall because it came with its own sink and mirror.

That gave her a bit of privacy as she alternated between two distinct emotions—unbridled rage and naked humiliation. One minute she would clutch both sides of the white porcelain sink and growl some version of "I'm going to kill him!" The next she'd forlornly look at herself in the mirror and say, "I can never show my face at school again."

Molly and Kiki did whatever they could to help. They let her get it all out and handed her toilet paper to wipe away any spit or tears. They also ran interference.

When one girl pounded on the door and told them to hurry up, Kiki instructed her to "Go pee in a cup!" (This was the moment when Allison and Molly officially decided that Kiki was all right.)

The two girls also tossed in bits of encouragement whenever Allison gave them an opening.

"It's not like he's your boyfriend," Molly reminded her. "This is all on him." (*And Dr. Ragans*, she thought, but wisely did not say.)

"Yeah," Kiki added. "For all most people know, you weren't even his date. You were just the unlucky girl standing behind him in line."

This calmed Allison a bit. "That really is true," she said. "He and I were just going *as friends*. Hell, we were all going *as friends*. We just rode in the same car. That doesn't mean anything. That's just carpooling. You can't blame a girl for being environmentally friendly."

She looked at them hopefully, and they did their best to sound convincing. "Totally." "Right."

Allison took a deep breath and in a very serious tone said, "There's one more thing I have to ask you."

"Go ahead, sweetie, just ask."

"Is there any vomit on my dress?" She did a quick turn and the girls scoped it out.

"All clean," Molly reassured her.

"Spotless," Kiki added. "Can't say the same for Dr. Ragans, though."

They shared a nervous laugh between them.

"Warren literally threw up on him, didn't he?" Allison asked. She had bolted the scene so quickly she hadn't gotten a full picture of what happened.

"Right on top of him," Molly said. "That suit is ruined."

Molly looked around and it dawned on her that this was the second time they had been in this restroom today. It was the same one in which Allison had calmed her down earlier during the walk-through.

"We are spending way too much time in this bathroom," she said. "Let's get out there and dance."

They finally left the handicapped stall and headed for the door. Then it hit Allison.

"I can't dance," she said.

"Of course you can," Molly said. "You're a great dancer."

"No. I don't have anyone to dance with." Allison's voice got more panicked as she talked. "I'm at prom . . . without a date."

This was a harsh reality. Warren may not have been much, but at least he was an actual person, someone sitting next to her at the table or moving near her on the dance floor. Now, she was all alone.

"You'll dance with all kinds of guys," Molly assured her, trying to convince herself in the process. "You've got lots of friends. And friends always dance together at the prom."

"Maybe later in the night. But for the first hour or so, everyone's going to be clinging to their dates." She sounded more panicked. "I'm just going to be sitting there all alone and people are going to walk by and stare and call me *vomit girl*."

Molly and Kiki shared a nervous look.

"Ben will dance with you," Molly offered boldly. "I'm sure he'd be happy to. And he's way better looking than Warren."

"He is kind of cute," Allison said, warming to the idea. "But it's your first date. I don't know if I could do that. I mean, if I already knew him, it would be one thing. We'd be dancing as friends. But we just met. It would be kind of weird."

Allison turned to Kiki, who was not particularly quick on the uptake.

"What about Peter?" Allison asked. "Would it be all right with you if I danced with Peter? Just once or twice."

Molly couldn't believe it. In the middle of this emergency, Allison was making her move on Peter.

"Of course," Kiki said, oblivious to any deception. "And you guys are already friends. So it wouldn't be awkward at all."

"Not at all." Allison beamed. "Thanks, Kiki, you're the best. I'm feeling better already."

Molly and Allison lingered for a moment after Kiki left.

"I cannot believe you," Molly said, jabbing her in the side. "Kiki was nothing but decent running in here to help you, and you made a play for her date."

"I didn't make a play," Allison protested.

"And what was with that whole 'vomit girl' act?"

"Too much?" Allison asked.

"Yes," Molly said. "Way too much."

Allison flashed a sheepish grin. (She knew it was completely uncool to undermine Kiki at the prom, but she just couldn't help herself.)

"It felt good, and I just kind of went with it," she rationalized. "Besides, aren't you the one whose senior quote is 'If we cannot find a road to success, we will build one'?"

"First of all," Molly said, "I hate that quote. You wrote it and turned it in for me. Secondly, I don't see how it applies to this situation."

"I'm just trying to build a road to success," she said, feeling a little bit guilty. (But only a little bit.)

Back at the table, Ben had successfully used the vomit story to keep most of the people away. But he was unnerved by a girl who kept looking at him. She was impossible to miss because she was dressed in a ruffled cancan dress and fishnet stockings.

Finally, she walked over toward him. (Technically, she slinked.)

Ben gulped. "Sorry, but the table's taken."

The cancan girl scoffed as only a full-fledged member of the Fletcher drama club could scoff.

"I'm not interested in your absurd table," she said.

He thought *absurd* was an interesting word choice and wondered if she knew what it meant or if she just thought it sounded good.

"I just wanted to leave a message for your friends Molly and

Allison," she continued. For dramatic effect, the cancan girl pulled out a chair. But rather than sit in it, she put one foot up on it to show off her fishnet stocking that much more. (This was a move she had mastered for a monologue that won third place in a dramatic interpretation competition.)

Knowing that nut-job girls were like Dobermans in their ability to sense fear, Ben did his best to remain cool.

"Tell them that Satine said, 'Ha, ha, ha.' (Each "Ha" was dripping with the dramatic flair of a true thespian.)

With that, she made a sudden turn that skillfully slid the chair back to the table as she started walking in the opposite direction. (Also from the dramatic interp.)

It was impressive. Frightening, but impressive.

After three steps, she stopped and looked back over her shoulder. *"Au revoir."* Then she continued to slink away.

"All right," Ben said aloud to no one in particular. "The girls at Fletcher have got their freak on tonight."

A few moments later, Molly and Allison arrived at the table.

"Sorry to abandon you," Molly said.

"Yeah," Allison added. "I didn't mean to have such a big freak-out the first time I met you."

"It's completely understandable," he offered.

"Where is everyone?" Molly asked.

"Peter is still with Warren, waiting for his parents to pick him up. Kiki went over to get something to drink. And some crackpot girl named Satine wanted me to tell you, 'Ha, ha, ha.'"

He did his best to imitate her dramatic tone. "I don't know what that means, but it kind of freaked me out."

Molly and Allison both laughed. "Her name's not Satine. It's Collette."

"Although she is a crackpot," Allison added.

"Why did she say her name was Satine?"

Molly and Allison did their best to explain. "Satine is the name of the character Nicole Kidman played in *Moulin Rouge!*"

"Collette is totally obsessed with the film. It's not just a movie to her. It's like her soul set to catchy pop tunes."

"She wanted 'Moulin Rouge' to be the prom theme," Molly continued. "But there was a fight and she threw a book."

"Not just any book," Allison chimed in. "*The Grapes of Wrath*. Hardback. More than a thousand pages."

Ben nodded. "I don't think crackpot begins to describe it. Why the 'Ha, ha, ha'?"

"She blames me because I'm the one who came up with 'Hollywood Dreams,'" Allison said. "I imagine she feels my date throwing up on the principal was kind of poetic justice."

Allison looked over at Collette and smiled. Collette faked a smile and waved back.

chapter FOURTEEN

The "Hollywood Dreams" theme was a huge hit. A steady stream of kids were lined up and posing for pictures next to the Hollywood sign. Others were scanning the floor to look for their names on the Walk of Fame. More than a few had decided to set up shop and do their dancing next to their own personal stars.

Even the deejay was getting into it. Along with his normal mix of dance, hip-hop, and pop tunes, he was playing movie songs ranging from the "James Bond Theme" to "It's Hard Out Here for a Pimp."

Clips from classic movies were being projected onto the wall next to the table where Rachel, Karolina, and Chas were sitting. The three of them made a game out of trying to be the first to name each movie. Rachel was still stinging from the way Victoria had treated her at dinner, but this was helping a lot.

Molly couldn't help but smile. Despite breaking up with her boyfriend and Warren vomiting on the principal, the prom was going great. She smiled as she and Allison carried a couple of sodas back to the table.

Just as they got there, the deejay put on a new song, and Allison started bopping the second she heard the pulsating beat. "My Love" was her favorite song by her favorite singer. Her crush on Justin Timberlake began when he was on the *Mickey Mouse Club*, grew during his time with *NSYNC, and became unbridled lust when (as she put it) "he became so freaking hot."

With Kiki's blessing, she hit the dance floor with Peter.

"That's really sweet of you," Molly said to Kiki after they left. "I think you saved her night."

"I'm glad to help." Kiki said it with a smile and she meant it. But she was not nearly as dim as everybody thought. She knew full well that Allison was hot for Peter. And she was okay with that. It's not like she and Peter were dating. Besides, she knew that at the end of the night, he'd be leaving with her.

Ben was surprised at how nervous he felt. He didn't know if that was a result of not knowing anybody there or if it was more because of how he felt about Molly.

He could already tell that he really liked her, and that was an emotion he hadn't felt much since he'd left Boston.

"You want to join them?" he asked Molly, motioning to the dance floor.

She nodded along to the beat while she finished off a swig of soda. "Love to."

As they headed to the dance floor, Ben instinctively put his hand back for her. She hesitated for a second and then slid her hand inside of his. Nice fit. It stayed that way until they found a spot on the dance floor near Allison and Peter.

Molly was pleasantly surprised to see that Ben was a decent dancer. Most guys either played air guitar or did a lame imitation of whatever was in the video. Ben just kept a steady groove doing most of his dancing from the waist up, his shaggy hair swaying with the beat.

"Where'd you learn to dance?" Molly asked, impressed.

"Mostly goofing around before and after swim practice," he said, suddenly self-conscious. "I don't know if I'd really call it dancing. It's more like bending with music."

"What about you?" he asked. "I'm guessing years of ballet lessons."

"Believe it or not, this is all self-taught," she said with a laugh. "Most of it picked up at middle school slumber parties over at Allison's house."

Ben laughed. "Can Mrs. Pirlo dance as well as she cooks?"

Molly shook her head. "Mrs. Pirlo can't do anything as well as she cooks. She provided the food; we got the moves from MTV."

They continued for a moment, and Ben tried to synch up his dancing with hers.

"Show me that one," he said about a move she was doing with her shoulders to the beat.

She reached over and put her hands on his shoulders to help him pick up the step. (Molly couldn't help but notice how muscular his shoulders were.) By the next chorus, he had it down, and they were moving in unison.

"Very nice," Allison called out from a few feet away.

Ben smiled back at her, making sure to keep up with the beat.

The night was taking on a surreal quality for Molly. She had spent months planning every little detail of the prom. And for all of the other couples who were there, it was unfolding exactly as she imagined.

But nothing was following the plan she'd laid out for herself. She was supposed to be dancing with Cameron. She'd even pulled rank and instructed the deejay to play *their* song as the final song of the night.

But Cameron was out of the picture and she was dancing with a guy she'd met just a few hours earlier. He was sweet and cute and just goofy enough to make her feel comfortable. Part of it felt great, but part of it was terrifying. For a girl used to keeping a schedule, this was all uncharted territory.

Uncharted didn't even begin to describe the situation Chas was in. He'd never been on a single date in his life. He didn't know what he was supposed to say or do. All he knew was what he got from movies, and he was pretty sure that *Superbad* wasn't a reliable guide to proper behavior.

Things seemed to go well when it was just him and Karolina talking. She knew how to make him feel relaxed. But as more and more people were around, he felt increasingly unsure of himself.

He was also surprised by how their arrival went. He knew that everybody would be amazed when he walked into prom with her. But he thought it would make him feel stronger, like he'd shown up all those people who'd made fun of him. It didn't. It just made him feel more out of place than ever.

As if the staring and whispering weren't bad enough, he had to deal with the dancing. (After all, the prom is first and foremost a dance.) This was a problem, because Chas didn't have the first idea of how to do it. And he could tell that Karolina was dying to hit the floor.

The more antsy she got, the more desperate he was to come up with excuses. (So far he had managed to nurse a six-ounce cup of Pepsi for four and a half songs. But eventually he would have to finish it.)

That's when he got a lifeline from one of the guys who normally tormented him. His name was Butch, and for the first time in his life, he treated Chas like he was a friend.

"Chas, my man, how's it hanging?"

Chas wasn't sure what this meant. "By force of gravity?" he guessed.

Butch laughed like it was hilarious. "Chas, you are too much. Listen, do you mind if I ask Karolina for a dance?"

Rachel shook her head, but Chas ignored her. He could not have been more relieved. "Mind? No. Why would I mind?"

The guy turned to Karolina. "May I have this dance?"

Karolina hesitated. She didn't want to leave Chas, but she really wanted to dance.

"You should dance," Chas said.

"If you're sure it's okay."

"It's fine, it's fine," he explained. "Go on out there. We can dance as soon as I finish my drink."

He smiled and waved as she went to the floor. The second she was away from the table, he started taking deep breaths.

"By force of gravity?" Rachel said, shaking her head.

Chas gave her a pained expression. He was doing the best he could.

"And here I always thought you were smart."

"I am smart," Chas retorted. "Gravity is how everything hangs. That's why I went with that answer."

"If you're so smart," she said. "Then why aren't you out there with her?" She pointed to where Karolina was seductively gyrating to the music. (She wasn't trying to be seductive. It just came out that way.)

Chas couldn't believe it. "How long have you known me, Rachel?"

She thought about it. "Since about third grade."

"That's right." He nodded. "And is there anything in the past decade that has given you the slightest reason to believe that I belong out there—with her?"

"It's not about the last ten years," she answered. "It's about tonight. What good reason do you have not to be out there tonight?"

"For one thing, I don't know how to dance," he explained. "For another thing—I don't know how to dance. And, oh yeah, I don't know how to dance."

"If I were you," Rachel said, "I'd learn really fast because dancing with her looks like it would be fun."

Chas looked out at Karolina and sighed. Rachel was definitely right about that. "If only dancing were easy," he said. "Like calculus."

After a moment, both of them burst out laughing.

Allison was having fun dancing with Peter, but it was hard to get him to focus. He kind of danced all over the place. And, like most of the guys with a pulse, he was a bit distracted by Karolina's writhing.

Allison had only a limited number of dances with him and didn't need to split time with the Olsen Twins.

"So what are your plans for after," she asked, trying to sound nonchalant. "You guys going to the lake?" (A lot of kids were heading out to an all-night party at a cabin on Lake Shelby.)

"I don't think so," Peter said. "It's going to get crazy down there and I'm not in a crazy mood. I'll probably just head back to Kiki's house. Maybe go for a swim. She's got an awesome pool with a hot tub."

Allison quickly pictured what Kiki would look like in a moonlit pool. It was a deflating thought.

"Won't her parents kind of be a buzz kill?" she said hopefully.

He smiled. "No. They went away for the weekend. It'll be just the two of us."

Allison missed a couple of beats while she recovered from this last bit of news. This was the problem with being Peter's confidante. He always gave her more information that she ever wanted to hear.

The song came to an end, and as a new one started, they headed back to the table. Kiki met them halfway, already moving her shoulders seductively to the beat. Unlike with Karolina, this was Kiki's intention.

"My turn," she said, brushing up against him as she walked by.

Peter smiled and gladly made a U-turn.

Suddenly Allison was all alone.

chapter FIFTEEN

8:31 P.M.

The limousine was quiet except for the faint sounds of "I Like It, I Love It." The radio wasn't on. It was Kirby. Whenever he got nervous, Kirby always sang Tim McGraw songs under his breath. He usually didn't even realize he was doing it. Jenna found it endearing.

Victoria didn't.

"Would you stop that stupid singing?" she barked at him across the backseat of the limo. Kirby clammed up and looked down.

Kirby was in line to become a third-generation firefighter. He'd already been through the junior program during the summer and hoped to attend the academy a month after graduating from Fletcher. So far, he'd been trained in CPR, basic rescue, and first aid. For a seventeen-year-old, he knew a lot of different ways to help someone. But none of his training gave him the slightest hint how to come to the aid of his good friend Matt as they rode along with their girlfriends.

When the limo reached the Legion hall, Victoria instructed the driver to keep going to her house.

"Why are we going there?" Matt asked.

"I want my father to look at your eye," she explained. "He's a surgeon. Maybe he can do something about it."

Matt was an easygoing guy. And he knew this was a big night for Victoria. But he was really getting tired of it all.

"You are making too big of a deal out of this," he said to her. "It's just a stupid black eye."

"Look at me," Victoria said. "Look at my dress, my hair, my makeup, my body. All of this has been meticulously prepared for this moment. Appearance matters. And when you are with me, you are part of that appearance."

Kirby took a deep breath and exchanged a look with Jenna. They knew better than to get involved. Rather than fight it, Matt just rode along, quietly looking out the window.

Without even realizing it, Kirby started to hum again until Victoria shot him a withering look. Finally the limo arrived at a huge house set back on a meticulously manicured lawn. Victoria got out first, followed by Matt. He leaned back in.

"You don't have to come in and deal with this," he told Kirby and Jenna. "Save yourselves."

Kirby wouldn't dream of letting him go in there alone.

"No way," Kirby said, climbing out of the backseat. He

looked his friend in the eye and said to him the same thing he said as they broke from every huddle during football season.

"I'll meet you at the quarterback."

Kirby winked, and for the first time since they'd left the country club, Matt smiled. On the football field the saying was part challenge and part promise. If both of them made it to the quarterback together, they had a much better chance of tackling him. Here, he was using it as a reminder that he'd be there for him.

"Dad," Victoria called as she walked through the door. "Where are you?"

"In my office," he answered.

The four of them walked into Dr. Sligh's office. Actually, it wasn't really an office. It was just the one room in the entire house that he had full control over. When they walked in, he was sitting in an overstuffed chair with his feet propped up on a table, watching the Golf Channel.

"You guys look great," he said. "But what are you doing home?"

Victoria was in no mood for small talk. "Look at this," she said, motioning at Matt's eye.

"Ouch," Dr. Sligh said. "What happened there?"

"Collision, sir," Matt answered. "At home plate."

Victoria's father smiled. "Did you get him?"

Matt gave him a confident nod.

"As if it matters," Victoria said. "Can you do anything about it?"

"What do you mean?"

"For my prom picture," she said, as if it were plainly obvious. "Is there some kind of medical something you can do to make him look normal?"

"There's not much you can do to treat a black eye," her father told her. "You can ice it for a while to constrict the blood vessels, but that's about it."

"I iced it on the bus for about forty minutes," Matt said.

"There you go," Dr. Sligh said. "Now you're just going to have to wait about a week or so for it to heal."

"That's just unacceptable."

The voice came from behind them and belonged to Victoria's mother. Even in her midforties, she looked as good as she did when she was crowned Miss Tennessee. She had been upstairs running on a treadmill when they arrived.

"Completely unacceptable," she continued. "What on earth happened?"

"I got hit during the baseball game, ma'am."

Mrs. Sligh turned to Victoria. "I thought I told you to have him miss that game."

"Yes, ma'am," Victoria answered meekly.

Kirby couldn't believe his eyes. He had never seen Victoria so submissive.

"Gee, honey, it's not like he can sit out of a game," Dr. Sligh chimed in. "He's the captain of the team."

One look from his wife silenced Dr. Sligh for the rest of the conversation. *You're on your own, kid,* he thought.

Mrs. Sligh was distracted for a moment. Something about Victoria's appearance caught her attention.

"Who put on your corsage?" she asked as she reached for it. "A brick mason?"

"I did," Matt said, starting to hold his ground.

She pulled the pin out and took it off. "Well, it's a good thing you play baseball better than you pin on a corsage," she condescended. "It goes like this."

She demonstrated as she went.

"You hold it at a slight angle, approximately four inches from the tip of the left shoulder."

Kirby looked over at Jenna's corsage and realized he had not done it right. He went to fix it.

"Don't," Jenna told him. "It's perfect."

He smiled and put down his hands.

"That solves the corsage," Mrs. Sligh said. "Now let's fix the eye. Follow me."

Victoria and Matt started following her.

"How are you going to fix it?" Victoria asked.

"With makeup."

Matt stopped cold.

"No, ma'am," he said. "I'm not wearing makeup."

Mrs. Sligh turned to face him. "Well, the prom queen is not posing for a picture with someone who looks like a thug."

All eyes were on Matt. "Then we'll have to find another way. Because I am not wearing makeup, ma'am."

The tension was almost too much for Kirby. Rather than look anyone in the eye, he absently looked at the prom invitation that he'd pulled from his jacket pocket.

Mrs. Sligh looked at Matt. "What way will we find?" she asked. "If you are too good for makeup, how will you make this right?"

Matt thought for a moment. He didn't have a clue. For a moment he considered wearing the makeup just to make it all go away.

That's when Kirby met him at the quarterback.

"Sunglasses," he blurted out.

All eyes shifted to him.

"What?" Victoria's mom demanded.

"Matt can wear sunglasses," Kirby said. "We've both got aviators. I'll wear a pair too. They'll cover the black eye."

"You're going to wear sunglasses to the prom?" she asked. "That's ridiculous."

Kirby held up the invitation. "The theme is 'Hollywood Dreams,'" he said. "Those movie stars wear sunglasses all the time. Inside, outside. It doesn't matter."

"Yeah," Jenna said, helping out. "It'll look cool."

Mrs. Sligh thought about it for a moment.

"Fine," she said. "That'll do for now. But when that heals, you'll pose all over again down at the studio. I wanted one taken with Victoria wearing her crown anyway."

"That's if she wins," Kirby said, suddenly feeling bolder. "No offense, Victoria, but my money's on Jenna."

Mrs. Sligh glared, but she didn't say anything.

Jenna smiled. She really loved Kirby, and this was one of the reasons why. He never backed down. She knew that he wouldn't grow up to be a rich doctor in a fancy house. But she also knew that he wouldn't hide out in his office because he was scared of his wife.

chapter SIXTEEN

9:04 P.M.

He hated the song so much he wanted to gag.

In fact, it was exactly because of syrupy love songs that A.J. usually avoided school dances. But tonight he was working, and the syrup was giving him exactly what he needed—a dance floor filled with slow-dancing, hormone-raged teenagers.

A.J. squatted down low in order to get the perfect angle with his video camera. Bodies moved in and out of the frame in front of him as he slowly zoomed in on a girl who had a single tear streaming down her face.

"Fucking perfect," A.J. said.

He was dressed in a black T-shirt and black pants and did his best to be invisible. This was not easy, considering he was lugging around a camera and kept getting in everybody's face as they celebrated.

A.J. had been making movies for as long as anyone could

remember. He was always talking friends and classmates into giving up chunks of their weekends to act in the digital shorts that he shot on video and posted on his website.

Molly and Allison had appeared as murder victims in one that spoofed horror movies. It was called *I Know What You Did Last Tuesday at 4:15*, and it imagined that the school's Latin teacher was also a serial killer who wore a toga and killed kids with a miniature of the Colosseum. (Mr. Longstreet had earned major props for dressing in a toga and pretending to bludgeon a few students in the film. He thought the story was hilarious.)

Next year A.J. was headed off to film school at the University of Southern California, and everyone was certain he'd go on to be a director someday. Before heading off to college, he wanted one last high school production. He was trying to figure out what it could be when Molly made him an offer he couldn't refuse.

She was trying to come up with the perfect prom keepsake when she thought of A.J. He could make a movie and they could sell it as a DVD. Not only would it make a great memento, but it was perfect for the "Hollywood Dreams" theme.

He held out with one demand. He wanted to have complete creative control. She agreed, and they even signed a contract.

A.J. was in heaven. For once he didn't have to convince anyone to act in one of his movies. He had a cast of hundreds, including all the biggest names in the senior class. For the documentary, he planned to make a bunch of different short stories and edit them together as one big piece.

This was going to be his epic.

After an hour of shooting, A.J. already had some incredible footage. Someone pointed out neither Marci Kent nor Claire Singer realized that they were both wearing identical dresses. He cleverly arranged for them to run into each other right in front of his camera. Their reactions were priceless. Marci called Claire a bitch, and Claire ran straight for the ladies' room.

When A.J. saw Collette's cancan dress, he knew he had a gold mine. Her interview went even better than he could have hoped as she went off on an incredible rant about a prom theme conspiracy. Then (with only a little prompting) she performed an entire scene from *Moulin Rouge!* in character. For this section of his film, he was going to edit her performance together with footage from the actual movie so it would seem like she was acting directly opposite Ewan McGregor.

The best footage had to be the shot A.J. got of Warren Sadler throwing up on Dr. Ragans. He was already working out that section in his head. He was going to call it the "Warren Report" and fill it with a bunch of eyewitness interviews like it was a news report. That's why he was headed over to where Molly was sitting with Ben and Allison. All three were at the scene of the slime.

"I'm shooting b-roll," he told them as he approached, shooting his camera. "Just act like I'm not even here."

"You mean act like we normally do," Allison joked without looking at the camera.

"That hurts, Allison. It really hurts," he joked. "I thought we were friends."

After he got a nice tracking shot around the table, he stopped the camera on Allison and zoomed in.

"Okay, Allison," he said. "What can you tell me about Warren Sadler's special greeting for the principal?"

It was a total ambush. Allison's b-roll smile turned into an evil glare.

"Perfect," he said. "Just the expression I was looking for."

Ben already knew he liked this guy.

From Allison's furious glare, A.J. panned over to Molly. "Can you tell us what Warren had for dinner?" he continued. "It was hard to tell with it spewed out over the floor like that."

"Stop! Stop!" Allison stood up and got in between Molly and A.J.

"Hey, you ruined the shot," he protested.

"Tell me you didn't get him throwing up on tape," Allison pleaded.

He stopped for a moment to put the camera down and smiled. "Full frame and perfect angle," he said. "I'll be the first to admit it was total luck. I was just testing the light meter for an inside reading and happened to be pointing the camera that way."

"You're not going to put that on the DVD, are you?"

A.J. laughed. "Are you kidding me? It looked like a Nickelodeon game show. I already sent one of the guys over to have it uploaded onto YouTube. That footage is going to generate some serious buzz."

Molly sank down in her chair. The night just kept getting worse.

"Speaking of YouTube," A.J. said to Allison, "I was kind of hoping I could shoot you watching the video on a laptop before you left tonight. It would really show the immediacy of the whole thing if we can get you watching it while the prom is still going on. I'm working on a whole technology-meets-tradition theme."

"Yeah, right," Allison said. "That's not going to happen."

"Don't say no," he said, picking up his camera. "Just consider it. It could be really special." He started to walk away. "I'll interview the rest of you guys later."

"It won't matter," Allison said. "Because my best friend Molly—the one who hired you for this job—would never let you put it in the DVD."

A.J. smiled and laughed. "She doesn't have a choice," he explained. "Read my contract."

Allison turned to face Molly. "You gave him a contract?"

"At the time, creative control didn't seem like such a big deal," Molly added.

"Just when you think it can't get any worse." Allison took a drink of soda, and things got even worse when she looked at Kiki and Peter slow dancing to the final strains of Edwin McCain.

Kiki was all over him.

It was more than Allison could bear. Then another slow song came on. It wasn't just any slow song. It was the ultimate slow song—Marvin Gaye's "Let's Get It On."

Ben was in an awkward spot. He felt like he and Molly were hitting it off, and he liked the thought of a slow dance. But he knew that would mean leaving Allison alone.

He leaned over and whispered. "You think it would be okay if we dance?" he said, motioning to Allison.

Molly wasn't sure. "I don't know," she offered.

"What? What?" Allison asked, cluing in to what was going on. "Why aren't you two dancing?"

"We didn't want to leave you all alone," Molly explained.

"Dance," Allison said. "I'll be busy plotting my revenge. It'll take some time, now I've added A.J. to my list."

"Are you positive?" Molly asked.

"Absolutely," Allison assured her.

Ben and Molly headed out to the dance floor. Neither of them was sure how close they should be while they danced. At first they started out about a forearm's distance apart.

For a few steps they didn't say a word. Molly just looked up at him and lost herself in his eyes. Then she moved closer and put her head against his shoulder.

They fit together perfectly.

Allison had shifted her attention from Peter and Kiki and was now filled with happiness for her best friend.

"Way to go, Molly."

And then it was over.

"Sorry to interrupt," A.J. said, breaking in after they had taken only a few steps. "One of the chaperones is hassling my lighting crew and I need you to help out for a second."

"Can it wait?" Molly implored him.

A.J. looked over to where a gym teacher was berating two guys with small stage lights.

"I don't think so."

She looked at Ben.

"You are the mayor of prom," he said.

"I'm sorry," she mouthed to Ben.

"It's all right," he said. "I'll go hang with Allison."

"Thanks," she said with a hint of regret.

Ben watched her head off in the other direction and then he returned to the table with Allison, who was shaking her head.

"So," he said. "Plotting revenge are we?"

She nodded. "I was wondering. If I hire a hit man to take out Warren *and* A.J., do you think he'd give me a two-for-one deal?"

Ben nodded. "You gotta figure he'd at least give you a discount."

She smiled.

"Besides," he added as he watched A.J. pull his date away. "If you add A.J. to the mix, I'll kick in some cash."

Allison laughed. They held up their sodas and toasted to their shared misfortune.

"Here's to revenge."

chapter SEVENTEEN

9:17 P.M.

The music reverberated through the limo, and Cameron rocked back and forth to the beat. "You like this song?" he asked his date, Jessie.

"I like anything you can move to," she said with a sly grin. "Is this the kind of music you play?"

"I'm more into hard rock," he said, trying to sound tough. "But it's prom night, so I thought we'd keep it mellow."

"Tell me about your band."

"I was in Date With Destiny, but I quit a few weeks ago," he said nonchalantly. "I'm looking for a group that's more interested in making good music than good money. For me, it's not about the commercialism. It's all artistic expression."

Cameron played the part of the tortured musician perfectly. Unfortunately, he didn't play the guitar nearly as well. He hadn't quit Date With Destiny; he'd been kicked out. It had nothing to do with artistic integrity and everything to do with his inability to play an entire song without screwing up. But he still had enough wannabe-rock-star cred to impress a sophomore like Jessie.

At least for a night.

Cameron hadn't planned to go to the prom after he broke up with Molly. But when he tried to get his deposits back from the limo company and the Ramada, they informed him that the money was nonrefundable. He'd mowed a lot of lawns to earn that money.

Screw it, he thought. *It's* my *senior prom too.*

It wasn't hard for a guy to find a last-minute prom date. In order to go, a student has to be asked by either a junior or a senior. That meant there were a whole bunch of sophomore girls just dying to get an invitation. Luckily, Cameron and the boys from Date With Destiny had found this year's sophomore class to be particularly slutty.

Jessie was more than willing to make sure his night was one for the memory books. He was good-looking and charming and had just a hint of bad boy to him.

It was just a hint.

Cameron wanted a bad-boy persona because he thought he needed it to be in a band. In truth, he fit in better with the kids in honor society than he did with the rockers who smoked behind the cafeteria during lunch.

That's why he clicked so well with Molly. They had never been friends before senior year because they hung in different circles and took different classes. But since their last names—Warfield and Walker—were so close alphabetically, they were always in the same homeroom. As a result, they had seen each other for about ten minutes a day every day since sixth grade. They always got along well and said hello whenever they'd run into each other away from school.

This year, however, Cameron decided to take yearbook. (He needed an easy A to boost his GPA.) Molly was the only one he knew in the class, and they started spending time together. She showed him how to lay out pages and crop pictures on the computer. In the process, she realized that the hard rocker was really a big softie.

They went from being acquaintances to friends. Cameron sat with her group at a couple of football games, and Molly went to a couple of Date With Destiny gigs to offer moral support.

Still, things were just friendly until both were part of a group that went to a yearbook conference. The conference lasted two days, which meant they had to spend one night at a hotel.

It was a night that Molly would always remember. She and Cameron ended up making out on a lounge chair by the hotel pool until about two in the morning. (Luckily, it was winter and no one else was by the pool.)

He figured it was a onetime thing, but it wasn't. That was the official beginning of their dating, and they were able to make a relatively smooth transition from being friends to being a couple. The key was that they were a couple who didn't have to spend every minute together. He still had plenty of time to practice with the band, and she got to chill out with Allison.

The problem that they hadn't been able to overcome was the prom. At first Cameron loved the fact that she was in charge of it. He sensed his impending ejection from the band and hoped he could save his spot by convincing Molly to book Date With Destiny for the big dance.

When that fell through and he was booted from the group, he suddenly had a lot of free time on his hands. Meanwhile, prom was getting closer and closer and Molly was getting busier and busier. Once-a-week meetings became twice-a-week meetings. Weekends suddenly included visits to see deejays and bands. (Cameron tagged along to see the band gigs in case anyone was looking for an extra guitarist.)

There was another conflict just beneath the surface of their relationship. Despite the fact that they began their relationship with a night of making out by a hotel pool, Molly wasn't always comfortable with where Cameron wanted to take the relationship physically. (Second base just didn't seem far enough for someone who fancied himself a rocker.)

Prom seemed like the perfect solution. Obviously, it was a huge deal for her. He decided to make it a huge deal for him, too. He'd already put down the money to rent a limo; he thought he'd take it one step further.

He figured it would be romantic for them to have their first night together after the prom. He couldn't afford a fancy hotel suite like some of the guys, but he thought the room at the Ramada was pretty nice. (It was even kind of romantic because that first night by the pool was also at a Ramada.)

Her reaction caught him completely off guard. He thought she'd love the idea. But she didn't. The fight was awful, and Cameron regretted it. He was into her. But musicians couldn't worry about girls in the past. He put his attention on the one cuddled next to him.

"Ever made out in the backseat of a limo?" he asked.

Jessie shook her head and bit her lower lip in a way that drove him crazy. Then she slid her hand down between his legs.

It was Cameron's ultimate rock-star moment.

chapter EIGHTEEN

10:12 P.M.

By the time prom reached its halfway point, there was no question that the person having the worst time was Gabe Magruder. Of course, no one actually knew his name. He was simply "the photographer."

Gabe had been assigned by the local photography studio to take the official portraits at the prom. He was given a corner near the entrance and set up a station where he could collect money and take the pictures. That, by itself, wasn't particularly hard. It was not too difficult to snap a picture of two people standing in front of either one of two backdrops. (One was a picture of the actual Hollywood sign and the other was the entrance to the famous Chinese Theater on Hollywood Boulevard.)

The difficulty lay in the fact that, unlike A.J., who had the freedom of creative control with his camera, Gabe was bound by the policy that "the customer is always right." (This was particularly difficult in a situation where the customer was in reality almost always wrong.)

So far he'd had a guy who was only five foot one demand he look taller than his five-eight girlfriend. Another girl asked him to take her picture in a way so that she could easily crop her date out of it. There were also not one but two couples who were now on the verge of breaking up simply because they couldn't decide which backdrop to use. (One girl claimed that their inability to decide was symbolic of much bigger problems. The other got mad when her boyfriend suggested they pose in front of the Hollywood Boulevard backdrop, and she said, "Why, because you think I'm a whore?")

Then there was Collette, the cancan girl. She refused to pose in front of either backdrop, insisting that her picture be taken in front of a Paris streetscape.

Gabe made the mistake of saying, "Believe me, if I had one, I'd be more than happy to do it. But these are the only two we've got."

That's when Collette announced that she had brought her own backdrop. It took twenty minutes to set it up and in the process put him way behind schedule.

As bad as Collette was, she was nothing compared to Queen Victoria. First, she cut in front of the line, claiming that, "Everyone knows members of the prom court are not supposed to wait in line."

Then she pulled out her own light meter. (Her mother taught

her how to dictate the proper light intensity for her complexion.) Finally, her boyfriend insisted on wearing a pair of sunglasses in the picture. (Gabe had no way of knowing that Matt thought it was equally as ridiculous.)

Meanwhile, A.J. was continuing to make his epic movie, providing stream of consciousness narration while he shot his footage. His current shot started with a close-up of one of his very best friends.

"Here she is, everybody," A.J. said as he focused on Rachel. "Ms. Rachel Buchanan, writer extraordinaire and everybody's surprise member of the prom court. Wave to the camera, Rachel."

Rachel waved and leaned forward so that her nose practically hit the lens.

"So, Rachel, where's your date?" A.J. asked, knowing full well that she didn't have one.

"I believe he's in the corner, making out with yours," she said with a smile.

A.J. laughed and panned over to Chas, who was sitting next to Rachel. "Next we have none other than Duncan U. Fletcher High School's very own computer prodigy. His birth certificate says Charles Montgomery, but we all know him better as . . ."

A.J. waited a moment for Chas to fill in the blank. Instead, he just had an embarrassed smile.

"Come on," A.J. prodded. "You can say it."

Chas considered it for a moment and then thought, *What the hell?* He looked into the camera and said, "Chas the Spaz!"

When he said it, everybody laughed, including him. It was oddly liberating. For some reason, saying it out loud weakened it.

"And you know why he's smiling, America?" A.J. said, continuing his narration. "He's smiling because check out who he brought with him to the big dance."

A.J. whipped the camera over to Karolina Olsen, who was looking particularly sultry in the dim lighting. "That's right. Chas the Spaz came to prom with the hottest girl in school. How'd he do it, Karolina?"

Karolina flashed a wicked smile and leaned into the camera. "He is absolutely amazing in bed."

Chas started snorting, and the rest of the table burst out laughing. A.J. laughed so hard that his camera shook, momentarily ruining the shot.

"Is that so?" A.J. gulped, trying to regain his composure.

"Actually Karolina, I do have a non-Chas-related question to ask you. As someone who is new to our country, what do you think of the whole prom thing?"

Actually, she had been thinking about this very subject all night. "I think it's interesting. Everyone's here for something different. Some people are here because they're looking for love and romance. Others want to show off how much money they have or how good-looking they can be. It tells you a lot about a person."

"And what does it tell us about you," A.J. asked her. "What are you here for."

"Strictly research," she said.

She didn't mean it bad, but it hit Chas right in the gut. She sensed that and turned to him. "Chas, I didn't mean . . ."

"No, it's fine," he said. "I'm here for research, too. It's no problem."

A.J. panned over to the next girl. Before he could say anything, she introduced herself.

"My name's Courtney."

"Courtney Townsend, right?" A.J. said.

She smiled. "That's right."

"I know your name, but not this handsome gentleman," he said as he panned to her date.

"This is my boyfriend, Ted," Courtney said. "He goes to a different school."

"Nice to meet you, Ted," A.J. said as he widened the frame so they both could be in the same shot. "Why don't you two snuggle in a bit?"

Courtney and Ted moved closer and looked to the camera. "How has prom been for the two of you?"

They looked at each other for a moment, and then she turned to the camera. "It's probably been the best night of my life," she said. As she talked, A.J. noticed a tear in the corner of her eye. This caught him by surprise. He let the shot linger for a moment before saying anything else.

"That's nice to hear, Courtney, Ted. Very nice."

A.J. wanted so desperately to know why it was such a good night. But something in him clicked and he realized that maybe it was too personal a question for what would ultimately be a joke-filled DVD. He let the shot linger for a moment longer, and when she didn't offer any details, he hit the stop button.

"Great," he said to everyone at the table. "I'll get out of your well-coifed hair for now."

As A.J. walked away, the table was oddly quiet. All eyes were on Courtney, who was suddenly a little embarrassed.

"I'm sorry if I got a little emotional," she said.

"Don't be," Rachel chimed in. "Don't ever feel sorry about that."

If this was the best night in Courtney's life, it was coming at the end of the worst year. Ten months earlier, her world had been turned upside down when her father was arrested for embezzling money from the law firm where he was a partner. He managed to avoid going to jail, but he lost his job, his benefits, and his license to practice law. Within a few months the family had exhausted almost all of their savings.

As bad as all of this was—and it was terrible—the worst part for Courtney was that her parents weren't doing anything to make it better. Rather than go out and get jobs, they were in denial about the whole situation. Earlier in the year, they'd lost their house and moved into a small apartment. Courtney had to work at a restaurant six nights a week just to help pay the rent.

While her friends at school were complaining about their outdated cell phones and their used cars, she was legitimately concerned that the power to their apartment might be turned off.

She did everything she could to keep this a secret from her friends at school. But a few of her teachers knew. Luckily, one of them told Mrs. White, the prom sponsor.

Mrs. White asked Courtney to come by her classroom after school one day. She explained that every year the school gave out about a dozen prom scholarships. These were completely anonymous. She was the only one who knew which students got them.

When Courtney realized that she was getting one of the scholarships, she started crying. She wanted to go to prom so badly. Mrs. White gave her an envelope with three gift cards. One was for the mall, so she could get a dress. Another was for one tux rental. And the last one was for dinner.

That night, Courtney and Ted never got close to a limo or a country club. She wore a simple but nice dress, and they ate dinner at the Olive Garden. They were there when the first song played and would stay until the end of the last dance.

It was the first time in a year that Courtney felt like her life might get back to normal one day. And when she said it was the best night of her life, she meant it.

chapter **NINETEEN**

10:27 P.M.

The dance floor was so packed that it was impossible to tell which people were actually dancing together. Ben was grooving with both Molly and Allison, and Allison was trying her best not to be distracted by the grinding going on between Kiki and Peter.

Rachel had finally ditched the table and was dancing with A.J., who had taken a break from shooting his video. Tired of waiting for Chas—who was still glued to his seat—Karolina had joined them, and A.J. and Rachel were both trying to dance without staring at Karolina.

Kirby, who preferred his dancing be done in a line while wearing cowboy boots, was doing his best to keep up with Jenna. Even Queen Victoria seemed to be finally having some fun as she danced with Matt.

Everyone was having a good time.

Then something caught Allison's eye.

"Shit!"

"What's wrong?" Molly asked.

Allison nodded to the door where Cameron and his sophomore bimbo were making an entrance. (Their backseat interlude had given him an extra bounce to his step.)

Molly sighed and stopped for a moment. She had prepared herself for the possibility of Cameron showing up, but it still stung to see him. She started dancing again, but her mood had shifted.

"What's up?" Ben asked, trying to figure out what was happening.

"My loser ex-boyfriend." Molly nodded over to where Cameron was introducing his date to a couple of his friends.

"How tacky is she?" Allison said, looking at Jessie.

"Extremely," Molly added.

Ben wasn't sure what he should do in this situation. He knew Molly had just broken up with her boyfriend, but he'd purposely not brought it up.

"Are you okay?" Ben asked.

"Yeah," Molly said, snapping out of it. "It's just annoying. I was kind of hoping I wouldn't have to see him tonight."

Pretty soon, she was dancing like nothing had happened. But Ben knew this could easily grow into a real problem. When the song ended, they all went back to the table. Ben was making sure to keep an eye on Cameron, who was doing the same to Molly.

When they sat down, Molly tried to get it out of her mind, but she couldn't. "I can't believe he came," she said to Allison. "He knows this is my night."

"It's okay," Allison reassured her. "It's not like you'll have to talk to him or anything."

"I wouldn't be so sure about that," Ben said, pointing behind them. Molly and Allison looked up to see Cameron coming toward their table.

"No freaking way," Molly said.

Cameron approached and Ben braced for the worst.

"Good evening, Molly, Allison," he said.

Allison rolled her eyes.

"I just wanted to stop by and say hello," he continued.

Molly gritted her teeth. "Hello, Cameron."

"I'd like to introduce you to my date," he continued. "This is Jessie." He thought they'd be really impressed by Jessie.

They really weren't.

"It's the junior-senior prom," Allison said. "Not the junior high school prom."

Jessie gave her a *fuck-you* look, which Allison gladly returned.

Throughout the exchange, Ben had kept his eye on Cameron. He knew that the real reason for the visit wasn't to show off Jessie. He knew that Cameron wanted to get a closer look at him.

"Hi, my name's Ben." As he said it, he stood up and unfolded his entire six-foot-two frame. By the time he was fully upright, he dwarfed Cameron by a good five inches.

"Nice to meet you, Ben," Cameron said with a cough. "I'm sure Molly's told you all about me."

"Nope," Ben said, just letting it hang there for a minute. "But we've been pretty busy making out."

Allison almost choked.

"Now, if you don't mind. We were in the middle of a conversation."

Cameron was a little stunned and more than a little intimidated. "Of course," he replied. "Like I said, I just wanted to say hello."

After an awkward moment, Cameron and Jessie left.

Molly couldn't believe it. Once they were gone, she turned to face Ben.

"I'm so sorry," he said. "I know I went too far there. I didn't mean to."

"No, not at all," Molly said. "That was awesome."

Allison couldn't stop laughing. "You are my new favorite person."

"So, you're okay?" Ben asked.

"Absolutely," Molly said. "In fact, I'm doing better than okay. I'm having a great time."

Ben flashed a killer smile. "Great. Because I am too."

Ben was a little surprised at how he reacted to Cameron. He hadn't figured he'd even care. But he was having a much better time than he'd imagined. Before Cameron's arrival, the only thing that had frustrated him was the fact that he and Molly still hadn't had a slow dance. He thought that would be an important signal of how things were really going. But every time they got close, something came along that interrupted them.

"What time is it?" Molly asked, suddenly sounding a bit panicked.

"Ten thirty-five," Ben said.

Molly flashed a pained expression. "I totally forgot. I have to go."

"Where?"

"I have to get everything ready for prom court," she explained. "The king and queen are crowned at eleven and I've got to make sure everybody knows what they're supposed to do."

"Okay," Ben said, nodding. "Is there any way I can help?"

"Nah," she said. "I just need to get the court together and go over everything with them. I'll do it as quickly as I can."

"Sure," Ben said, trying not to sound too bummed. "You know you still owe me a slow dance."

Molly smiled. She liked the sound of that. "I always keep my word," she said. Then she turned to Allison. "Keep an eye on him for me, okay?"

"You bet," Allison said. "He's my new favorite person."

"See you guys in a few," Molly said as she rushed off. When she was just a few feet away, a slow song started playing.

"Perfect," Ben said. "I can't seem to catch a break with the slow songs."

"I know the feeling," Allison replied, looking out at Peter and Kiki.

Ben's gaze drifted out toward Molly, and he was lost in thought for a moment.

Allison leaned over to whisper something to him. "She's worth waiting for."

He smiled and looked at her. "I know."

A few tables away, Karolina sat down next to Chas. She had a sense of urgency about her. She reached over and turned Chas's chair so that he was looking right at her.

"Why won't you dance with me?" she demanded.

"What?"

"Why won't you dance with me? You haven't asked me one time."

Chas started getting a little uncomfortable. He decided to be honest. "I don't really know how to."

"Then why did you ask me to a dance?"

Chas thought about it for a moment and looked her right in the eye. "Strictly research," he said, repeating the line she had given during her on-camera interview with A.J.

Karolina felt bad about what she'd said. In a way, it had been a truthful answer. There was a Jane Goodall part of her that wanted to observe everything up close but still remain separate from it. But she was also realizing that if she really wanted to know what everyone was going through, she'd have to actually go through it too. She couldn't just see it. She had to feel it.

Karolina didn't say anything for a moment. She wanted to choose her words carefully, which was not always easy to do in a second language.

"It was an awful answer," she explained. "A bad joke. But it's not true. I'm not here for research. I'm here with you. You're my prom date, Chas. That means you're supposed to dance with me."

It was getting harder for Chas to play this off. "You've been dancing all night. With all kinds of people."

"But I don't want to dance with all kinds of people," she tried to explain. "I want to dance with you."

This almost pained him. "Why?" he wanted to know. "Why would you want to dance with me? I'm Chas the Spaz and you're . . ."

"What, the Olsen Twins?" she said, referring to the nickname for her breasts. "You think I don't hear people talk about me? These guys don't want to dance with me. They want to dance with my boobs. They want their buddies to see them on the dance floor with the hot Swedish chick."

This was becoming Chas's greatest nightmare. He was on the verge of crying. "I don't know how to dance," he explained. "Why are you doing this to me?"

She smiled. "Because you called the embassy to learn Swedish. And you had to suck on your inhaler just to knock on my door. And you chased after Rachel when no one else would."

Karolina smiled and gave him a slight touch on the arm.

"You even thought enough to bring the DVD of my favorite movie. You're the one that I want to dance with."

Suddenly, Karolina had an idea.

"Wait here," she said. "I'll be right back."

She disappeared for a moment, and Chas considered bolting out the door.

"Don't you dare," Rachel said, knowing full well what he was thinking. "A very hot—and very cool—girl wants to dance with you. That's a rare and valuable thing."

"It is if you know how to dance," he explained. "If I go out there and make a fool of myself . . ."

"What?" Rachel laughed. "People are going to make fun of you? They do that already. How much worse could it be?"

He considered this. "That is a valid point."

"And if you don't go out there, you'd regret that for a long, long time."

Karolina hurried back to the table. She was bubbling with excitement, a huge smile on her face.

"My research is over and I'm ready to boogie," she announced. "Chas, will you be my date to the promenade?" (It was the same way he had asked her.)

Chas knew that he could no longer ignore this. He pulled his inhaler out of his pocket and took a hit. Then he steeled himself. "Yes, Karolina. It would be the highlight of my life to be your date to the promenade."

She smiled. "So, does that mean you'll dance with me?"

He gritted his teeth and nodded. "Even if I make a fool of myself."

"I think that's kind of the whole point," she explained as she took him by the hand and led him out onto the dance floor. He couldn't help but notice that some people were already pointing it out.

"This is really going to be awful," Chas said to himself but loud enough for Karolina to hear.

She laughed. "We'll be awful together."

The slow song ended, and the deejay took the microphone for a moment. "I hope the Hollywood dreams are coming true for all you Fletcher Senators out there." There was a hearty round of applause.

"I've got another movie classic for you all. It's a request, and if I'm reading this right, it's dedicated to Chas the Spaz from the Olsen Twins."

The crowd roared and Chas just shook his head. He knew he was about to go down in flames big-time.

The music started playing, and much to his surprise, Chas recognized the song.

The deejay finished the intro. "From the movie *Grease*, here is "You're the One That I Want.'"

Karolina smiled. "You said your mom made you watch it a hundred times."

He nodded.

"Then you should know the dance by now."

As the music played, Chas did his best to remember the different dance steps from the scene in the movie. He stumbled a little, but the amazing thing was that he got a few of them right.

Rachel stood up on her chair and gave him a whistle of support. A few other people started to surround the two of them.

Chas just kept dancing through the embarrassment, and by the time they reached the chorus, he was fully channeling John Travolta. It wasn't that he was a good dancer. (He wasn't.) It was just that for the first time in his life, he didn't care. He was so lost in the music and so lost in Karolina that it just seemed right. (Of course, it helped that Karolina was supplying a fair share of Olivia Newton-John sexiness on her side.)

By the end of the song, no one was dancing but the two of them. Everyone else had encircled them and was clapping to the beat. When the pair finished, there was a huge round of applause.

"I thought you couldn't dance," she said.

He laughed. "So did I."

Chas smiled and Karolina gave him a big hug. He was exhausted, excited, and exhilarated. And, strangely enough, he didn't feel the slightest need to use his inhaler.

chapter TWENTY

10:43 P.M.

Molly had gathered everyone on the prom court and they were all crowded into the office along with the principal (who had gone home and changed into a new, vomit-free suit) and the prom sponsor, Mrs. White, who was talking to everybody.

"First," she said, "let me congratulate all of you for being selected to the prom court. It's really an honor, and I hope all of you are having a great night."

Rachel looked over at Karolina, and they shared a smile. So far it had been a very good night.

"I also want to give a huge thank-you to Molly Walker, who has organized every last second of this dance. Molly, you have done a stupendous job."

The court members all gave her a round of applause—even Victoria. She had already shifted into her "nice mode." (Her mother had trained her that it was important to project humility whenever she won something. Actually feeling humble was insignificant, but projecting it was essential.)

"And, with that, I'll turn the floor over to her." Mrs. White nodded at Molly, who checked her clipboard to go over each step of the ceremony.

"In about fifteen minutes we'll crown the king and queen and we just want to make sure that all of you know where you're supposed to stand and what you're supposed to do.

"First, Mrs. White will announce the name of the prom king. If she calls your name, walk right over to her and she will place the crown on your head."

"Remember to bend over," Mrs. White added. "I'm only five three."

Molly continued. "She will give the king a microphone so that he can say a few words."

"Keep it brief and keep it clean," the principal interjected. (A few years earlier the winner was so excited that when he took the microphone, he said, "This is fucking awesome!")

"Once the king is done talking," Molly picked up, "Dr. Ragans will announce the queen. If he announces your name, go over to him and he will place the tiara on your head."

"I think I'm taller than all of you," he said. "So you don't have to worry about bending over."

"That's a relief," Karolina said, adjusting her top. This brought a big laugh from the room.

"The queen will also get a chance to say a few words."

Jenna looked over at Victoria and could tell that she was already practicing what she was going to say.

"At this point," Molly picked back up, "after the announcement, the king and queen share a slow dance to a song of the queen's choosing."

Victoria looked over and winked at Matt.

"Halfway through the dance, the rest of the court will join them on the floor and then all of your classmates will follow."

"That's so cool," Karolina said, excited by the sense of tradition.

"Have all the queen candidates turned in their song choices?" Mrs. White asked.

"I've got them right here," Molly said. "I'll make sure the deejay gets them."

"Great," Mrs. White said. "You guys have about ten minutes back here to freshen up and then we'll have some fun. Good luck to you all."

The court members all thanked her and started to mill around. Victoria and Jenna headed to the restroom to check themselves in the mirror. Rachel and Karolina came over to talk with Molly.

"So, who's the guy I saw you with?" Rachel asked with a devious smile.

"His name is Ben, and he goes to West High," Molly answered.

"He's cute," Karolina said.

"A definite upgrade from Cameron," Rachel added.

At the time, Ben certainly wasn't feeling like an upgrade. He was sitting with Allison, both of them stranded without dates. (In fact, he had spent more time that night with Allison than he had with Molly.)

"Maybe she's just not into me," he said.

"Wrong," she told him. "I can tell. She's really into you."

Ben chewed on it for a moment. "I just don't know."

"Don't get discouraged," Allison told him. "Good things come to those who wait."

"You mean like the way you've waited for Peter."

"Ouch," she said. "You don't hold back, do you?"

"Sorry."

Allison shook her head. "Don't be. I'm the one who has totally let it slip away. It's my fault that we're not together."

Peter and Kiki left the dance floor and came over to the table. "I think we're going to call it a night," he said.

Allison started to panic.

"Don't you need a ride?" she asked.

"No," Peter explained. "Kiki's best friend, Stacey, is about to head home. They live on the same block, so she can give us a ride."

"You would take another ride over the lame-o?"

Peter laughed. "Hard as it is to believe."

Allison was desperate to stall them. "What about king and queen? Don't you want to see who wins?"

Peter rolled his eyes. "The last thing I need to see is another coronation of Queen Victoria."

"Okay, then," Allison said, disappointed but unable to do anything about it. "You guys have a great time."

Just then the deejay played the classic love song "At Last" by Etta James.

It was one of Ben's all-time favorites. "I love this song," he said.

"So do I," Kiki said.

Suddenly Ben saw a chance.

"I know you guys are leaving," he said, "but Molly's been pulled in every direction tonight and I'd really like to get at least one good dance in. Would it be possible for me and Kiki to dance to this song before you go?"

Kiki was game. She'd had an eye on Ben all night long. She looked over at Peter, who was always easygoing about everything.

"Sure," he said.

"Thanks so much," Ben said.

Ben took Kiki by the hand and led her to the floor. As he did, he gave Allison a look that said, *It's now or never.*

Peter sat down next to Allison.

"He's a pretty cool guy," he said, looking at Ben. "Think things will work out with him and Molly?"

"Peter," she said, gulping and totally ignoring the question. "Would you dance with me?"

"Sure," Peter said, oblivious to how important this was to Allison.

They got out onto the floor, and she leaned in close to him. It was dark, but he thought he could see some tears in her eyes.

"Is everything all right?"

She just buried her head against his chest and nodded.

Peter didn't know what to make of it, but he just started dancing. They stayed like that for a little bit and then she looked up at him.

"First of all, let me tell you how sorry I am to do this to you," she said.

"Do what to me?" he asked, more than a little confused.

"I know you're about to go and have some great prom-night sex by a pool with a super-hot girl. And I know that's every guy's fantasy."

Peter tried to interrupt, but it was useless.

"And she's not just hot, Peter. She's actually pretty decent. She's been nice to me all night long, and considering that, it really sucks that I'm doing this."

"You still haven't said what you're doing," Peter reminded her.

"I am telling you that I love you, Peter. I have always loved you. Ever since tenth-grade English. I've always loved you and never had the courage to say anything. Because I thought it was better for you not to know and still be my friend than it would be for you to know and never want to talk to me again."

Peter was overwhelmed.

"And I just wanted to make sure that you didn't leave here tonight without knowing that."

She stood up on her toes and gave him a kiss on the cheek just as the song came to an end.

Peter was speechless, and before he could even respond, Kiki and Ben were there.

"Thanks for the dance," Ben said to Kiki.

She winked. "My pleasure. Molly doesn't know what she's missing."

Then Kiki turned to Peter. "Come on, we better go. Stacey's waiting."

Peter was still dumbfounded. "Yeah, right," he said.

"Have a good time, guys," Allison said, putting on a brave face.

"Yeah," Ben added. "It was great meeting you both."

"Nice to m-meet you, Ben," Peter stammered.

He wanted to say something to Allison, but he had no idea what it should be. Before he could think of something, Kiki led him away, and they disappeared into the crowd.

"Did you say it?" Ben asked quietly.

"You bet your ass I did," Allison said with a smile. "I said it all."

"But he still left with her."

Allison looked at him and nodded. "That's okay. Now it's his mistake and not mine."

Ben smiled. "Want to join me at the loser's table?"

"I'd love to."

Molly was stuck in the back waiting for the prom court to get ready. She would have died if she'd known how much prama was unfolding out on the dance floor. She'd been after Allison for years to say something to Peter. Now she'd missed it.

She was also missing a chance to get to know Ben. Things had started out pretty good and gotten better through the night. But Cameron's arrival had ruined everything. She couldn't get him out of her mind. He was the most serious boyfriend she'd ever had and seeing him had reminded her that she was not over him yet.

"It's really a great prom, Molly."

Molly closed her eyes for a second and then turned to see Cameron.

"What are you doing back here?" she demanded.

"Nothing," he said, holding up his hands innocently. "I just saw you come back here, and I wanted to make sure that I told you how nice everything is. I know that you worked really hard on it. I'm having a great time." (He neglected to mention a big part of his fun had been a backseat quickie with Jessie.)

"Thanks," she answered warily.

"It's also a lovely dress," he added.

"Listen, Cam. I'm not really in the mood for you to suddenly be nice," she told him. "I have some work to do. I have to get the prom court ready for the crowning of the king and queen."

Cameron laughed. "Of course you have work to do. There's always work to be done," he said.

Molly tried not to take the bait, but she just couldn't resist.

"Don't blame what happened to us on the prom," she said. "That is completely unfair."

"I know," he said. "It's nobody's fault but mine. I screwed it up. I screwed it all up."

"You did," she said, tears forming in her eyes. "You absolutely did. And now you come here with that tramp."

"There weren't a lot of choices out there," he said, trying to excuse it. "You sure found yourself a large young man."

"He's nice," Molly said. "He's nice and he treats me great."

"Which you completely deserve," Cameron said. "I'm glad to hear it." (If Cameron played guitar as well as he faked sincerity, he'd be playing in front of sold-out arenas.)

Molly was exasperated. "Why are you here, Cameron?"

"I just wanted to say, if there's anything I could do to make things better—anything at all—I would do it. I would make it all better."

Molly took a couple of deep breaths. Before she could answer, Mrs. White came into the hallway.

"All right, everybody," she announced. "It's time for royalty."

Molly looked at Cameron.

"I have to go."

chapter TWENTY-ONE

11:04 P.M.

Molly was a total wreck when she came out onto the stage. She didn't know what she should do about Cameron or Ben. So much had been focused on this one night that she'd lost all perspective. She didn't know what she thought about anything.

Luckily, she had a schedule. And whenever she was in trouble, Molly always found comfort in her schedules.

When the song ended, Molly signaled the deejay, and he turned on her microphone and the stage lights.

"Hello, everybody. I'm sorry to interrupt your dancing. I hope that everyone is having a great time tonight."

There was a loud roar, and Molly appreciated that her hard work had not gone to waste.

"Now, before we get on with the big announcements, I wanted to take a moment to thank some of the key people who made this night possible. First of all, there is the prom committee, nine young girls who did the work of hundreds. Let's hear it for them.

"As most of you have already noticed, I'm sure, A.J. Quinn has been shooting a lot of video tonight, and he'll be producing a DVD of the evening, which anyone can purchase. If you're interested, there are order forms on the table in the back corner," she said, pointing toward it.

"Now, for the moment we've all been waiting for, I'd like to introduce Mrs. White, the prom sponsor."

Mrs. White walked out onto the stage and took the microphone. "Let's hear it for your prom committee chair, Molly Walker."

There was more applause, and Molly waved embarrassedly as she retreated from the stage.

"First of all, we'd like to announce the prom king," she said. "Gentlemen."

She introduced them one by one, and they walked out to the center of the stage. Normally, these were the coolest guys in school, but in this situation they weren't exactly sure how to stand, and there was a general awkwardness about them. (Somewhere in the crowd, Chas was pleased.)

Mrs. White held up an envelope and waved it dramatically. Even though she was the only one who already knew the results, she opened the envelope for the pure theater of it all. "I would like to congratulate your prom king—Matt Hall."

The students broke into applause, and the other guys on the court all gave him slaps on the back.

Matt came over to Mrs. White and felt like a total dork

when he bent over so she could put the crown on his head.

"Congratulations," she said.

"Thanks."

She handed Matt the microphone. He always knew what to say one-on-one with a teammate, but he was clueless as to what he should say to such a large group of people.

"I am honored and would like to thank everyone who voted for me. If you hadn't, I wouldn't be out here feeling like the biggest horse's ass in the world."

Everybody laughed.

"Sorry, Dr. Ragans," he said, remembering what the principal had said. "Horse's butt."

That brought even bigger laughs.

Dr. Ragans came over and took the microphone from him.

"Now it is my great pleasure to introduce you to the young ladies who have been nominated for prom queen. The first one is not only the best-dressed girl on campus, but also one of the nicest—Jenna Copeland."

Jenna walked onto the stage and was greeted by a fair amount of applause.

"Next we have an exchange student from Stockholm, Sweden, who has already blended right into the Fletcher family—Karolina Olsen."

Backstage, Victoria cringed when she heard the loud round of applause. She knew that Karolina had a real chance of pulling the upset.

"Our third contestant is the president of the senior class, captain of the cheerleading squad, and was your homecoming queen—Victoria Sligh."

Victoria walked out with the practiced precision of a pageant veteran. She totally ignored the lukewarm welcome and smiled and waved as if there were thunderous applause.

Dr. Ragans smiled before he read the last name. Like the students, he had been pleasantly surprised about her inclusion on the list.

"Finally," he said. "A girl who is Ivy League bound—the one and only Ms. Rachel Buchanan."

Rachel walked out onto the stage and was greeted by the largest ovation of all. She was stunned. It made her go from extremely self-conscious to unbelievably self-conscious.

"Ladies and gentlemen, your prom queen candidates."

There was one last round of applause. Rachel didn't know what to make of any of it. She tried to take mental notes for her column, but it all was getting more and more overwhelming.

The principal signaled them all to get closer and they held hands. (Rachel was at one end holding Karolina's hand, while Victoria was at the other end holding Jenna's.)

Unlike Mrs. White, the principal had no idea what the results were, so he was more than a little excited to open the envelope. When he read the name, he was caught off guard and actually let out a little laugh.

He looked over at Mrs. White, who smiled. She'd known all

day who'd won, and she'd been dying for someone else to know.

Dr. Ragans turned to the girls and then to the crowd. "Congratulations to your prom queen—Rachel Buchanan."

The entire room went silent as everyone made sure they heard what they thought they heard. Finally, someone broke the silence.

"That is fucking great!"

It was A.J., working his video camera from the front row. It had been a completely natural reaction, and the second he said it, the entire crowd burst into applause.

Victoria was trying her best to keep her calm. Karolina was one thing—at least she was hot—Rachel was completely unacceptable.

Rachel was equally disbelieving. She wasn't sure she'd heard right until Karolina started jumping up and down and hugging her.

She was too stunned to move, so the principal came over to her.

"You aren't serious," she said to him.

Dr. Ragans smiled. "Congratulations, Rachel."

First he helped her put on the prom queen sash and then he put the tiara on her head.

With each step, the crowd clapped louder and louder. And with each step, Victoria got more and more angry.

"I don't know what to say," Rachel said as he handed her the microphone. "This has got to be a mistake."

"It's not a mistake," Karolina shouted gleefully.

Finally, it all hit Rachel, and she started to cry. All she could say was, "Thank you, very much."

At this point, Rachel was just looking for a shoulder to cry into. She got it from Mrs. White, who came over and gave her a big hug.

After a few moments, Mrs. White took the microphone and addressed the crowd.

"Now, it is tradition for our king and queen to dance. For half the song, the floor is all theirs and then everyone can join in."

Rachel stepped out to the center of the stage and turned to Matt. He approached her, but something stopped him. It was Victoria, holding his arm.

"No," she said sternly, bringing a hush over the crowd.

Matt couldn't believe it. "What are you talking about?"

"I'm talking about you and her," she said. "You are not dancing with that dyke."

Rachel was horrified. Everyone was horrified.

But just as he did on the baseball and football field, Matt Hall knew just what to say.

"Well, I'm certainly not dancing with a bitch like you."

With that, he pulled his arm free and headed over toward Rachel.

Victoria had a look of total disbelief. It was an expression that no one had ever seen on her face before. But luckily, it was all captured on tape by A.J. Quinn, who had the perfect angle.

He zoomed in tight on her face—her world at an end.

A.J. savored every moment. "Fucking awesome," he said gleefully.

chapter TWENTY-TWO

11:11 P.M.

Rachel was horrified. She wasn't positive, but she was pretty sure Victoria Sligh had just outed her right in front of the entire prom. Everything was a blur as she looked out at the faces of her classmates. They all had shocked expressions, but she couldn't know for sure which part of it all had shocked them.

She just wanted to disappear.

Then she turned and saw Matt coming toward her. He had a huge smile, and it made her feel much better.

"Congratulations," he said. "May I have this dance?"

Rachel was still in shock, but she managed to nod.

He led her out to the center of the dance floor, and the deejay started playing the song she had written down on the off chance she won.

It was "Purple Rain," by Prince.

"You're playing my song," Matt said to her.

She buried her face in his chest and cried. They were the only ones dancing, so all eyes were on them.

After about thirty seconds, she finally looked up at him.

"You know, what she said, what she called me."

"Yeah," Matt said.

"I think it may be true," she said. She thought for a moment and corrected herself. "Actually, it *is* true."

This was the first time she had ever admitted it to anyone, and she was terrified of what he might say.

"Does that mean you don't want to dance with me?"

"No," she said with a snort. "Of course not."

Matt looked down at her. "Does that mean you don't want to grow old with me and raise my children?"

He had broken through her tears, and she let out a quick laugh. "Yes. It means that."

Matt smiled. "Well, it's a good thing that I only asked you to dance."

She had almost forgotten about all of the people surrounding them. She was totally focused on Matt.

"Although," she said. "If I were into guys. I think you'd be my type."

Matt laughed. "You are such a tease."

They both laughed, which relaxed all of the people who were watching them.

"You know," Matt whispered, "I voted for you."

Rachel couldn't believe it. "Are you serious?"

He nodded. "Yeah. I think you're the perfect person to be the prom queen. You winning this is one of my favorite moments of the year."

She wiped away the last of the tears and looked up at him. "Do you know what my favorite moment was?"

"This?" he said expectantly.

"No. It was that hit you laid on the quarterback in the game against Terry Parker. I never thought that guy was going to get up."

Matt smiled. "That was a good hit." Then something about the song caught his attention. "Wait, wait, this is my favorite part."

He started singing along, and she just laughed and sang along too as they danced. An avalanche of purple balloons cascaded from the ceiling and covered them and the dance floor. Within moments they were joined by their classmates.

Molly was so caught up in the spectacle of what happened that she almost forgot about her dilemma. But from her vantage point on the stage she could see both Ben and Cameron. She was having a great time with Ben, but it was just a first date. She knew that nothing might come of it. She'd had a serious relationship with Cameron, and if he meant what he'd said, maybe that relationship wasn't over.

She did the one thing that had worked consistently all day. She hurried into the girls' room. There she found her familiar spot in the handicapped stall and locked herself in to think.

She made it all of five seconds before there was a knock on the door.

"Are you going to let me in?" Allison asked.

"Go pee in a cup," Molly said, half-joking and half-serious. She waited a moment and slid the latch open.

"What is going on?" Allison asked as she walked in.

"Cameron wants to get back together," Molly said.

Allison laughed. "So?"

"So, he's special to me," Molly exclaimed. "He's like the only serious boyfriend I've ever had. We split up during a period of great pressure, and I'm not sure we shouldn't still be together."

"You're serious?"

"Yes."

"What about the bimbo he brought here tonight? Does he just get a free pass for that?"

Molly was frustrated. "I don't know. Do I get a free pass for bringing Ben?"

"How can you compare them? He's great—smart, funny, caring. What's there to get a pass for? And, by the way, he really likes you."

"He does?" Molly asked. "Are you sure?"

Allison nodded enthusiastically. "We've had a lot of time together tonight. He may have mentioned it on several occasions."

Molly tried to figure out the best way to decide. "You know, I've spent a lot of time planning this prom. I've planned out every little detail for every person. By the way, how great was it that Rachel won?"

"Greatest moment ever."

"Anyway. I've planned out every little detail for every person. And each time I planned it, the night ended with Cameron and me dancing the final dance to our song. Amazingly, that can still come true."

Allison shook her head. "You and your freaking plans and schedules and calendars. Why do you do that? Why does everything have to go according to plan?"

Molly couldn't think of an answer. "I don't know," she said. "But it feels right when it does."

"There's just one thing I want to tell you—"

Just then somebody knocked on the door to the stall. Allison and Molly exchanged a look and both said, "Go pee in a cup."

"As I was saying," Allison continued. "There's just one thing that I want to tell you. In the last year, the happiest I have ever seen you was in a rare unplanned, unscripted Molly moment. It was tonight when you and Ben started to slow dance to 'I'll Be.'"

"It was 'Let's Get It On,'" Molly corrected.

Allison smiled. "I know that. I just wanted to see if you did."

Allison left her there to solve the rest on her own.

A few moments later, Molly came out of the restroom. Both Ben and Cameron were standing nearby.

She still didn't know what she wanted to do.

The deejay started to talk into his microphone. "This is our last song of the evening, so I want to see everybody on the dance floor."

It was "I Will Remember You," by Sarah McLachlan—Molly and Cameron's song. The one she had pulled rank to get the deejay to play last.

She looked at both of them. "I'm sorry. I don't know what to say."

Ben smiled. "If that's the case, I'll say it. Good-bye."

Ben turned and headed for the door. Molly's instinct was to follow him, but Cameron swooped in and took her by the arm.

"Molly, they're playing our song."

She watched as Ben walked through the door and disappeared into the night.

"Come on, Molly," Cameron said. "It's the last dance."

Cameron led Molly onto the dance floor, and they danced to the last half of "I Will Remember You." It was exactly how she had planned the evening to end. Amazingly, everything was back on track.

She was miserable.

chapter TWENTY-THREE

11:33 P.M.

Ben took long, loping strides as he hurried through the parking lot. This made it hard for Allison to catch up. She reached him right as he got to the lame-o.

"That's it?" she demanded. "Good-bye?"

When Ben turned, she could tell that he was upset.

"What was I supposed to say?" he asked.

"I don't know," she offered. "Something like, 'Hey, I really like you'? Or 'Don't go off with that loser'?"

"You don't get it," Ben shot back. "She didn't pick me."

"She didn't pick him either," Allison pointed out. "But you just gave her up."

Ben was too frustrated to say anything. He just opened the door and got inside. Allison got into the passenger's seat.

"What now?"

"You're my ride," she reminded him.

"Sorry," he grunted. "I forgot."

When he started the car and didn't kick her out, Allison knew she had about five minutes to save the relationship.

"You need to understand," Allison said as they rode down the street. "She's been under a tremendous amount of stress lately. She hasn't been herself."

They reached a stoplight and he turned to her. "I really appreciate what you're trying to do," he told her. "I just don't think it was meant to be."

Allison rode along quietly for a while. "You know, I used to think that Peter and I were meant to be," she offered as the car neared her house. "I was just certain we'd end up together. So, I never said a thing and because of that I never got a chance to find out if we really were meant to be or not. Don't be an idiot and wait around for fate like I did. If you really like her, you've got to let her know."

He stopped the car in front of Allison's house.

"It was really nice meeting you," he told her. "Thank your mother again for the delicious dinner."

Allison got out of the car and leaned back in the passenger window. "I'm sorry it didn't work out."

They shared a smile and she walked toward the house. Just as she got to the door, Ben called out to her through the car window.

"Allison?"

She stopped and turned around. "Yeah?"

"If I were to chase after her," he said. "Where would I go?"

She smiled. "She should still be at the dance for a few minutes. She's supposed to make sure the cleanup gets under way."

"Thanks," he said as he pulled off down the road.

"Good luck!" she called out before adding to herself, "At least someone might have a good prom night."

She walked up the steps to her house, and through the window she could see her mother walking across the family room.

She waited up. Which part do I tell her first?

"Look who's back," her mother said as she came over to the door to greet her. Allison was expecting a hug, but instead her mom was giving her a mini inspection.

"What are you doing?" Allison asked.

"Just making sure he didn't throw up on you, too."

Allison couldn't believe it. "You already heard? Tell me you didn't see it on the Internet."

"No," Mrs. Pirlo answered. "He told me."

Allison looked over and saw Peter coming out of the kitchen carrying a soda.

"You finally made it," he said, smiling.

Allison couldn't believe it. "You're here."

Peter nodded. "Yep."

Suddenly she got nervous. "You didn't bring Kiki with you, did you?"

He shook his head. "Nope. I kissed her good night and thanked her for a lovely evening."

Allison was trying not to tear up. "And then you came here? To see me?"

"You're good at this," he said.

Mrs. Pirlo knew it was time to get out of the way. "Now, if you two will excuse me, I'm going to go to sleep. In my room, on the other side of the house. Where I won't be able to hear a thing."

She came over and gave Allison a kiss on the forehead. Then she leaned over to Peter and whispered, "I always knew you'd figure it out."

Mrs. Pirlo left the two of them and headed up the stairs to her room. When she was gone, Peter turned to Allison.

"I am so mad at you," he said.

"I know. I ruined your night."

"No, stupid," he said. "You ruined my year. Think of all the dates we could have had by now."

"I have," she said, half laughing, half crying. "Some of them in minute-by-minute detail."

He laughed and came over to her. "But mostly, I'm mad because you told me that you loved me and didn't wait to hear my answer."

She looked at him, not believing it was all happening. "Well, what's your answer?"

He leaned over and kissed her. It was without question the best kiss she'd ever gotten. She kept her eyes open the whole time. She didn't want to miss one thing.

chapter TWENTY-FOUR

11:40 P.M.

The song ended, Sarah McLachlan stopped singing, and suddenly the prom was over. Molly had spent so much time planning it that she was almost in a state of disbelief that it was over. Not only that, but her head was still spinning with everything that had just happened. Somehow, she was with Cameron. And the more she was, the more she thought it might be a mistake.

"Come on, baby," Cameron said, taking her by the hand. "Wait until you see the limo." (Suddenly, he seemed less sweet and remorseful.)

"I'm supposed to make sure the cleanup gets started right," Molly protested.

Cameron gave her an exasperated look.

"You're right," she said. "They'll be fine. Let's go."

Molly didn't even think to ask what had happened to Jessie, Cameron's actual date.

As they walked out the front door, a few random people thanked Molly for such a fun night. She answered them, but she was mostly on autopilot. She was on the lookout for either Ben or Allison.

When they got to the parking lot, they had to wait in a line as the limos came to pick everyone up.

"Congratulations," she said as Rachel passed by.

"Thanks so much," Rachel answered. She was getting into Chas and Karolina's limo along with Matt, who had now joined their group.

While they waited, Molly snuck around back to check the secret parking spot they had used. It was empty.

"He really left," Molly said to herself, full of regret.

Cameron opened the door to the limo and led her in.

"You're going to love this thing. It is fully tricked out."

"It's big," she said as they climbed into the backseat. It was really nice, but Molly was surprised to realize that she liked the lame-o better. At least it had character.

"Where are we going?" Molly asked.

Cameron paused, unsure what to say. "Well, I thought we'd go to the Ramada. But just to chill with some friends. You don't have to do anything you don't want to do."

Cameron's limo pulled out of the parking lot just as Ben got back to the Legion hall. Not that it would have mattered; he had no way of telling one stretch from another.

The parking lot was a total zoo. Ben scanned the crowd for any sign of Molly or Cameron.

Next he went inside where there were still some stragglers. The only one he recognized was Collette, the girl with the *Moulin Rouge!* fascination.

"Well, well, look who the cat dragged in," she said in her unmistakably dramatic way.

He was really not in the mood for Ms. Psycho, but she was all he had.

"Have you seen Molly?" he asked her.

Something about the way he said it let her know that he was in pain. And pain was something she could relate to.

"Yes," she answered, dropping her act completely. "But it was about ten minutes ago. I think she was headed for the door."

He took a deep breath.

"Was she with Cameron?"

Collette nodded. "I'm afraid so."

This hit hard. "Thanks," he told her.

He knew there was no way of guessing where they were headed. All night he'd heard about different after-parties. They could be anywhere.

Then he saw a second face he definitely recognized. It was Jessie—Cameron's trampy sophomore date. He hurried over to her.

"Hey, you're Cameron's date, right?"

She scoffed. "I was."

"Do you know where he went?"

"He said he had some big fancy hotel suite. Turns out it was just a room at the Ramada."

Ben smiled. He'd seen the Ramada earlier. "Over on Highway Fifty?"

"That's the one."

Ben thanked her and rushed out to his car. He had no idea what he would do when he got there, but he realized that he had to try something.

He figured he had only one real shot. If they stopped to get a bite to eat on the way, he could beat them there. That way, he could confront them in the lobby. (There was no way he was going to knock on the door to a hotel room.)

He practiced different confrontation lines while he drove:

"Molly, there's something you need to know."

"I shouldn't have walked out earlier."

"Hey, you, hands off my date."

He pulled into the hotel parking lot but didn't see any sign of them or a limo.

He still had hope.

He parked his car and rushed into the lobby. He needed to find out if Cameron had checked in or not.

"Good evening, welcome to the Ramada Inn, how can I help you?"

"I need to see if one of your guests has checked in."

The woman behind the counter smiled. "What's the name?"

"Cameron."

She typed the name into her computer. "I'm sorry. There's no Mr. Cameron staying here."

"No. Cameron's his first name," Ben said. "I don't know his last name."

"I'm sorry," the woman said. "That's the only way I can look it up."

Ben thought for a minute. "Maybe you remember checking them in. He's wearing a tux. He looks kind of squirrelly."

None of this was registering for the woman.

"The girl is much more memorable," he added. "She's real pretty, about five foot seven, with curly black hair and eyes that are kind of green, kind of brown, depending on how the light catches them."

The woman smiled at the description. "What was she wearing?"

"Killer dress," he said. "Dusty white and antique rose."

"It's dusty rose and antique white," a voice behind him said.

Ben spun around and saw Molly sitting on the couch in the lobby. He'd run right past her when he came in.

"What are you doing here?" they both asked in unison.

"I'm waiting for my mom to come pick me up," she said.

"What about Cameron?"

Molly paused for a moment. "I finally realized that he's just not good enough."

Ben smiled. "Any chance that I'm good enough?"

Molly nodded. "In fact, you're exactly the right amount of goodness," she said. "I just can't believe you came back."

"Well, you did promise me a slow dance."

"I did," she said. "And I always keep my promises."

Ben looked around the lobby. "Should we dance here?"

"No," she said with a devious smile. "I can do better than this."

They waited in front of the hotel for Molly's mom to arrive. Ben kept his distance while Molly explained the situation to her mother. Then they headed back to the lame-o.

By the time they reached the American Legion hall, everyone was gone and the lights were all off.

"What are we doing here?" Ben asked.

Molly pulled a set of keys out of her purse and dangled them in the moonlight. "One of the perks of being the mayor of prom."

Ben smiled. They entered through a side door and made it out into the main hall. Moonlight streamed in through some skylights.

"Don't turn on the lights," she said. "We don't want anyone else to know we're here."

"Good idea," he answered.

For music she pulled out an old radio she'd seen earlier in the office. They found a spot on the dance floor in the shadow of the Hollywood sign and just lost themselves in each other. There was nothing to distract them. No one to interrupt. It was just the two of them and some scratchy music.

They danced for a couple of songs without even saying a word. Then Ben broke the silence.

"Molly, there's something I've been wanting to ask you for a while."

"What is it?"

"Well, I'm worried you may not like it."

She steeled herself for the question.

"My school is having its prom in two weeks, and if you're not doing anything, I'd love to take you."

"That depends on the transportation. What are we talking here? A limo?"

"Not a limo," he said. "Something much better. It's called a lame-o."

They both laughed and then they kissed and continued dancing through the night.

epilogue

Two weeks later

Prama—a documentary by A. James Quinn—was
quickly edited and sold well among the Fletcher student body. Much to the director's dismay, the final
version did not include footage of Warren Sadler throwing up
on the principal. Dr. Ragans reminded A.J. that while he might
have creative control, the principal still had control over all student grades and transcripts. There have been reports of bootleg
"director's cut" versions complete with the "eruption," although
these reports have yet to be verified.

In a surprise coupling Collette Martin and Cameron Warfield
hooked up the night of prom. She was impressed with his musical background, and he was impressed with the fact that she
was a girl. He is currently trying to master the *Moulin Rouge!*
songbook for guitar, and she is working on what she hopes will
become a successful one-woman show called *Satine*.

Cameron is still searching for a band that is less concerned with making great money and more concerned with making great music. (He figures they'll be less concerned with actual ability.)

Warren Sadler managed to avoid getting suspended from school when he convinced the principal that it wasn't alcohol that caused him to throw up but food poisoning. Dr. Ragans did give his parents the dry cleaning bill, which they happily paid.

Kirby aced the entrance exam to the state firefighting academy. In the days leading up to the test, he got some extra math tutoring from his new friend Chas Montgomery. There were a few points during the test when Kirby felt the need to hum Tim McGraw, but nobody around him seemed to mind. To celebrate, he took Jenna line dancing. Chas was invited but claimed to have a previous engagement.

Jenna got an acceptance letter from a prestigious school of design. She's not sure how she's going to pay for it, but she's applying for scholarships, and her mother told her they'd definitely find a way.

Victoria Sligh was not seen or heard from much in the two weeks following the prom. Her family took a sudden vacation to Vail, after which she claimed to be dating a college sophomore who plays on the University of Colorado football team. Mrs. Sligh came down to the school and demanded a recount of the prom queen vote. Dr. Ragans laughed before kicking her out.

While they are not girlfriend and boyfriend, Karolina Olsen and Chas Montgomery have gone out on a couple of dates. For Karolina the dates are purely for fun—no research value. There has even been talk of Chas visiting Sweden for a week during the summer. As a going-away present before she heads home, she's going to let him get to second base. Just to be safe, she's also going to make sure he brings his inhaler.

Fletcher played its final baseball game of the season, beating Terry Parker 5–2. Matt Hall had a single and a double and caught two base runners stealing. It marked the last time he would put on the purple jersey of the school he loved. Not many fans made the thirty-minute drive from Fletcher to see the Saturday-morning game. One of the few who did was Rachel Buchanan. She cheered wildly throughout the game and afterward gave Matt the triple high five that he normally reserved for his closest teammates. When the team celebrated by playing "Purple Rain" one final time, it had new meaning for both Matt and Rachel. Both sang along at the top of their lungs.

Rachel did not write a "My Life as a Prom Queen" column for the school paper. At Matt's urging she decided that her last column should not be about pretending to be someone else—it should be about admitting who she was. Like most of Rachel's columns, "My Life as a Gay Teenager" was humorous and thought provoking. It caught the attention of the editor of the local newspaper. He not only reprinted it on the editorial page, but he also offered Rachel an internship with the paper.

Rachel's mother was so proud she had the article framed and hung it on the wall next to a picture of Rachel and Matt during their dance.

Allison and Peter have spent most of the past two weeks making up for lost time. Tonight they are planning on going out for dinner and a movie.

First, though, Allison is helping her best friend, Molly, get ready for the West High prom. Unlike their last prom adventure, this one has been preceded by no breakdowns or freak-outs. Molly decided to skip the salon and let her mother do her hair.

She has no idea what will happen between her and Ben, and for the first time in her life, she is fine with not having a plan. She's just going to take each day as it comes. Although, she considers it a good sign that when he arrives to pick her up, Ben only has a pin-on corsage.

ABOUT THE AUTHOR

Jamie Ponti was born in Italy, grew up in Florida, and went to college in California. A writer and television producer, Jamie attended a total of four high school proms and college formals. The picture above was taken at one of the formals, a hastily arranged blind date much like the one at the center of *Prama*. Twenty years and two kids later, the happy couple is still smiling.